HEROES

DEACON'S LAW

RJ SCOTT

Love Lane Books

Deacon's Law (Heroes #3)

Heroes #3
Copyright © 2017 RJ Scott
Cover design by Meredith Russell
Edited by Rebecca Hill
Published by Love Lane Books Limited
ISBN - 978-1978135697

ALL RIGHTS RESERVED

DEDICATION

Always for my family.

With grateful thanks to Meredith for her beautiful cover, Rebecca for fixing stuff, Rachel for sorting me out, and my army of wonderful proofers for their hard work.

CHAPTER 1

Winter 2014

"What the hell are you doing, Rafe?" Deacon asked, and edged closer, carefully.

Rafe was too near the edge of the lake in the darkness, and he didn't want to spook the man. He'd been watching him from a distance, but when Rafe stepped closer to the inky depth of water, Deacon had to step forward. The lake was icy cold and deep here, and ice collected around the edges. The crystal in the pale moonlight would have been beautiful but all Deacon saw was danger.

"Looking," Rafe murmured, and stepped even closer. The lake was around Rafe's feet now, and Deacon realized that Rafe had stopped on a piece of ground that jutted into the ice.

He wanted to tell him to move away, but that wasn't his job.

Neither of his jobs.

"What are you looking at?" he asked, and casually stepped closer; just out of grabbing distance, but close enough to try to stop him if he jumped into the lake.

"The ice is pretty here," Rafe murmured.

He sounded contemplative, quiet, serious, and Deacon didn't like that one little bit. He'd once talked a jumper off a ten-story building, and Rafe's voice had that faraway quality that spoke of a decision made and an action that needed to be carried out.

"Come back," he said; more ordered. He had to stay in character for now, but what if Rafe decided that he was jumping? What did Deacon do then? No one said he had to care about Rafe, but he did.

This was week three, and he'd seen Rafe bullied, and ignored, and seen him close his eyes to it all. He hadn't seen a family who had welcomed a bereaved nephew and cousin into the fold. All he'd observed was that Rafe shouldn't be there.

"What?" Rafe asked dreamily. Deacon had to think to remember what he'd asked.

"Come away from the edge," he reworded the instruction. "You don't want to slip in."

Rafe let out a sharp bark of a laugh. "What if I do?"

What?

"Rafe—"

"You could get me some skates, and I could glide on the water. I've never done that before; we didn't have a lot of iced-over lakes in Miami. I'm surprised there is one here in California."

"It won't last," Deacon said, and stepped a little closer. "Only on the coldest nights and just at the edge, but the water would be cold if you swam in it."

He saw Rafe's full-body shudder. "I don't want to swim in it. It's a horrible, scary lake, so deep you can't see the bottom, and who knows what I'd find down there if I did."

The lake was on Rafe's uncle's land, a natural crack in the terrain with an icy spring that fed it. Deacon had a feeling there were a lot of things in its depths that were never meant to be found again.

"I've skated on a frozen pond," Deacon said, a little desperately – anything to get Rafe's attention. "Back in Massachusetts, the pond in our town wasn't deep, but it spread a good way, and it would ice over when it got cold."

After a moment's pause Rafe spoke. "When was that?"

Yes, he was talking back.

"When I was a kid. I used to go skating with my best friend, Mac."

"No, I mean, how long did it… was it… I don't know what I mean."

Shit, this doesn't sound good.

Deacon carried on. "There was always September first, and it was all rust and gold as far as the eye could see, and then you'd have the snow and ice and the cold of winter."

Rafe shivered and wrapped his arms around himself, and Deacon took a cautious step forward. *Keep talking.*

"One day, maybe I'll go visit there again in the Fall, and wait for the snow and cold so I can skate again. See my family, visit with friends."

Rafe nodded, as if he was actually listening. "Friends are good," he muttered, and then the tension slipped away from him and his arms fell to his sides.

What happened next was Deacon's worries come to life. Rafe turned to face him, slipped on the ice that had crept onto the grass on the bank, and began to slide toward the water.

Deacon grabbed for Rafe, any part of him, getting a solid hold of his arm and hand and yanking him back, stumbling away from the water and tumbling to the ground, Rafe a solid weight on top of him.

He didn't want this. He didn't want sexy, intriguing Rafe sprawled over him, laughing like an idiot. He didn't want Rafe at the lake, or even in the same fucking state as his asshole uncle and cousins. Trying to extricate himself from the pile of limbs he was tangled in was useless. Rafe was a dead weight, and seemed to be content being wrapped around Deacon.

"Kid, you need to move," he muttered, willing away the arousal that was zipping through his body.

Rafe snorted another laugh. "You know I'm twenty-three, right? Legal in every state, or at least I think so."

"Get off me." Deacon tried to buck him off, but Rafe was hard against him, and heavy, and clinging like a freaking limpet.

"I know you've been looking at me," Rafe murmured, dipping his head so they were close enough that Deacon could simply lean up a little and they would be kissing.

Remember the goal.

"Kid, Jesus," he said, in an exasperated tone, which was heavily at odds with the arousal he was feeling at having gorgeous, sexy Rafe slumped over him.

But the tone didn't work, and Rafe wasn't moving.

In fact, he ramped the whole thing up so it was worse than before. He peppered Deacon's face with kisses; small touches with each word, explaining why he wasn't a kid and Deacon should kiss him back.

For a while – seconds, hours, he didn't know – he tried to get away from this maniac with the kissing and the laughter, and then abruptly things changed.

In a smooth move, he twisted so it was Rafe on the ground under him, abruptly quiet and looking up at Deacon, his eyes wide.

"Deacon?" he asked, his tone wary.

And Deacon kissed him.

He held Rafe's hands to the icy ground and kissed him, pressed him hard into the mud and explored Rafe's sexy, pouty mouth with a thoroughness that had him near to coming in his pants as they rocked against each other.

This kiss was deliberate and needy and the want of it had been building ever since he'd arrived at the Martinez place.

"Deacon!" a voice called in the darkness, and Deacon was off Rafe and up on his feet within seconds, holding out a hand to help Rafe stand. He brushed himself off, and Rafe moved back and away into the shelter of the nearest tree.

"You got your eyes on him?" Chumo asked, his tone accusing.

"Following him around the lake," Deacon reported, then turned away from Rafe's cousin, the least psychotic of them. "Need to go."

Chumo spun on his heel as though that was enough for him. His dad or brother had likely told him to go look for Rafe, and his job was done. When Chumo left, Rafe stepped back out with a soft laugh.

"That was close," he said, coming to a stop right next to Deacon, his hand brushing Deacon's arm.

Deacon rounded on Rafe. "Don't fucking touch me," he spat. Rafe blinked at him, startled, hurt in his expression.

"I saw your eyes," Rafe murmured.

"Let's get back." Deacon turned to walk away, but Rafe didn't follow.

"And I felt that kiss," he added.

"I'm not repeating myself," Deacon snapped.

This time he sensed Rafe following, and they made their way back to the main house. Rafe said nothing and went to his room quietly. Only when Rafe was in his room did Deacon ever feel truly able to deal with his real mission; finding evidence to tie this family to terrible crimes that destroyed lives.

This family, and possibly Rafe.

Rafe closed his bedroom door behind him. He wouldn't need to come out of his room now until morning, and if he was lucky he could avoid his family and get to school without incident. Of course, Deacon would be right on his tail all the way to college, but he could handle that.

Or at least, he had been able to until just now.

Now? Well, hell, it would be a hundred kinds of awkward, facing Deacon after that kiss and then Deacon shutting down on him so abruptly.

For a second, Rafe had seen naked need in Deacon's eyes, and then one word from Chumo and Deacon had pulled down the mask that was his hard-man persona. Rafe was convinced there was more to Deacon; he just didn't know how to reach the man.

But the need for it burned in him, and he had no clue why. Lusting after one of the bad guys was going to compromise everything he was there to do, but that wasn't enough to stop him. He was losing his freaking mind.

Lying back on his bed, he stared at the ceiling, and the unsettling feeling of being watched was back again. He hated this place, hated his family, just wanted to be back in Miami with his dad and his stories of how his mom had died. The only place he could find them again was in his memories, and he closed his eyes, thinking of one single day when everything had been okay. Of course, he'd never known his mom – she'd died a few weeks after he was born – but his dad had kept her memory alive with photos and stories. She'd danced, or so his dad had said, danced with crazy happiness in their kitchen, danced slow and crying when she was emotional; to hear his dad tell it, she'd been a whirlwind of motion. Every photo he had of her, she was smiling back at Rafe, but he didn't have the photos here. They were boxed up in storage along with the rest of his life.

Was I really going to walk into that water?

The thought of it, of stepping into the ice, had been right there in his mind. He imagined the grief of losing his father slowly floating away as he sank to the bottom, and he rolled onto his front, his face buried in his pillows. The tears he cried were hot and fierce, but he didn't sob, or shake; his grief was his alone.

I don't want to die.

He hated his uncle, hated him with everything he had. He'd hated him as a child, and now, as an adult, when the grief wasn't overwhelming everything else, he hated Arlo with every fiber of his being. His dad had been convinced that Uncle Arlo was evil.

"Arlo hated me for marrying his sister," his dad had always said when whiskey had loosened his tongue. "But I didn't care. My Santanna was everything to me, and when she gave me you, I couldn't have loved anyone more. We didn't need her family." And then he would correct himself. "We don't need her family."

"Why did I even leave Miami?" Rafe muttered, and kicked the corner of the bed, wincing when the bed didn't give way but his foot did.

He should have stayed in Miami, in the house he'd shared with his dad, surrounded by photos of his mom; hell, he should have listened to his dad and left well enough alone.

"Stay away from your mother's brother," he'd said over and over before he died. "That's the bad side of the family. Your Uncle Arlo and his sons, your cousins, they are bad men."

Growing up, he'd begun to associate the word "bad" with his uncle and his two cousins, Felix and Chumo. They were all the way over the other side of the country in California, and that was pretty much all that Rafe had known.

Until his dad had been dying and he'd told Rafe everything. Said he'd written everything down, located people who'd seen things, had evidence that Rafe's uncle had killed Rafe's mom. Beaten her to death. He'd gone to confront Arlo. He was sorry. He'd fucked up.

What Rafe heard had made his blood run cold. It had also had him organizing his last semester in California, citing that he needed to be with family now his father was dead. The lie sat uneasily with him, but his old college had been okay with it all, the bereavement counselor positively beaming as she ticked all the right boxes about this newly orphaned young man finding family to take care of him.

Grief at losing his dad, and a new acid of hate that was forcing its way into his heart, was what had sent him here.

His dad had been his everything. The mild-mannered man had taken him to peewee baseball, the dentist, school, helped him with homework, and not once had he spoken about his life in Cuba, or his family.

Not until that last week.

Not until the car had hit him, and he'd laid dying in a hospital, and he'd told Rafe what he'd lived with for so many years.

So many secrets that had changed Rafe's life forever.

He rolled onto his back and stared up at the ceiling again, considering how long he could keep up the pretense. He should have handed everything over to the cops, but then his dad would have been pulled into the mess posthumously, and his good name was the one thing that was left now of Héctor Ramirez; that and Rafe's memories of his dad. He had details in his head of his mom's supposed car accident, a statement from the first cop on the scene; she'd been run off the road just outside the town he was in now. Her car had been shoved off the road, but that had never made the official statements. The cause of the accident had been covered up; she'd been visiting her brother in California and she'd died tragically after she'd lost control of the car. Nothing about the dents that had to have been made by another vehicle. Everything had been covered up, or so his dad had thought. And the accident itself a cover-up for her being beaten to death by her brother.

His dad had sworn that was true.

Rafe didn't know what to think.

Then there was the hit-and-run responsible for his dad's death, less than a week after the only visit he'd ever made to visit his brother-in-law in California.

"I went to make him tell me what he'd done," his dad had told him. "He told me he'd beaten his sister, as if it was okay, as if he was entitled. But I saw evil in his eyes. Always look into a man's eyes, Rafael. It's up to you to find out what he did."

The burden of this weighed on Rafe. He wanted to know how his mom had died, who had killed his dad. But now, here in this house, he was losing his mind in the biggest way.

His Uncle Arlo had, of course, welcomed *his beloved nephew* with open arms, which Rafe had counted on – Arlo was big on family, and hadn't batted an eyelid at his nephew living with him when Arlo was the only family Rafe had left. Particularly when Rafe had said nothing about his parents other than the normal exchange of superficial grief statements.

"I miss them," Arlo had said with great feeling.

"Me too," Rafe had said, keeping everything inside him.

One thing Arlo hadn't welcomed him into was the business. Nope, everything had been pushed away, and he'd been kept separate, even so far as being assigned a bodyguard, *for his own protection.* Deacon had been hired to keep an eye on him. Or at least that was what Rafe thought. It was no accident that Deacon had turned up a couple of days after he had, nor that he was always everywhere Rafe went.

Rafe just needed to play the long game and get enough evidence together to back up his dad's observations, see if they were more than just the ramblings of an old man, and then he could hand the whole lot over to the police.

Then he could make his uncle pay.

CHAPTER 2

Deacon should have known that Rafe wouldn't stay out of trouble. He'd stayed in his room the rest of the evening, but the next day he was back to college, and when he came home his whole demeanor had changed. He had this look of determination on his face, and that was only going to end badly.

He was only a few minutes ahead of Deacon going upstairs to his room, but that would clearly be enough to mess things up.

He would have been right behind Rafe, but Bryan stopped him on the stairs.

"Can we talk?"

He was a barman, but he was also more; he used the drugs that Arlo sold. He was a good enough kid, laughed a lot, but he was trapped there by more than a job; he relied on being paid in heroin.

"Later," Deacon said, and tried to move past.

"Please, Deacon…"

"Later, find me later," Deacon said, and moved past him, straight up the stairs.

He heard the words long before he saw the people speaking them.

"Little homo," the voice dripped with sarcasm and hate.

Felix, the older twin, arrogant asshole.

"He's not worth it."

Chumo, the peacemaker, younger twin.

The third person around the corner wasn't talking. Rafe never talked, never fought back, just closed his eyes and let it happen. And why wouldn't he? He was shorter than Felix, not weak but certainly not hopped up on whatever the hell steroids Felix took to make himself bigger. He probably knew that his only chance was to play possum, close his eyes and hope the words, and sometimes violence, stopped.

"You wanna tell me what you were doing in the office, homo?" Felix snapped, and there was the sound of a fist meeting flesh. Deacon wanted to step forward right there and then and get Felix bloody and unconscious on the ground.

But he couldn't.

He had to hear what the answer to that question might be. He clearly hadn't been the only one to notice that Rafe spent a little too long with his nose in places it shouldn't be. Idiot man.

Still nothing from Rafe – not a single word. Deacon fought the instinct to go charging around the corner, knocking the twins on their asses and blowing the cover he was trying so hard to keep solid. From the first look, Rafe had gotten under his skin, with his innocent eyes and his serious expression.

And then last night had happened, and everything had changed in one single moment of insanity. One stupid-ass kiss and he'd realized that Rafe could be the very thing that destroyed two years of work.

"Felix, stop." Chumo actually telling his brother to stop? That was new.

"Fuck you," Felix snapped, and there was another sound of someone being hit. "Fucker's all up in business that doesn't concern him."

Deacon wasn't gaining anything by standing there, apart from growing his already guilty conscience and fighting the desire to rescue Rafe and drag him right away from this toxic vipers' nest. He stepped around the corner as casually as possible, sizing up the situation in a few quick glances. Rafe with his back to the wall, on the floor, his knees drawn up, his face buried in his hands. Next to him a bag was ripped, books strewn on the floor, and notebooks open at random pages full of words and doodles.

"Felix, your dad is downstairs," Deacon lied, and left it loose-ended, implying that possibly Felix's dad wanted him, which would clear him from the corridor and the quieter Chumo would go with him.

They didn't move. If anything, Felix looked more determined, toeing at Rafe and cursing under his breath. Deacon tensed and thought on his feet. He dropped to a crouch next to Rafe and gripped his hair, tipping his face up.

"What'd the little fucker do now?" he asked, seeing the split lip that was bleeding copiously down Rafe's stubbled chin. Rafe's eyes were tightly shut, and for a second Deacon wished he'd open them so that he could look right into them and reassure Rafe about who he was and what he was doing. He gentled his hold on Rafe's hair and saw a faint flutter of his eyelids, but no sign of the pale green irises beneath.

"Caught him in the office," Felix said, posturing, his arms crossed over his chest. Felix wasn't just a bullying asshole, he was his daddy's son, and he was out to kill someone one day. Not that it hadn't crossed Deacon's mind that Felix could actually already be a killer. Too many missing people in this city for it not to loop right back to the psychotic bastard hating on his own cousin.

Deacon sighed theatrically. "I'll take care of it," he said, and his tone brooked no argument.

"I want to know what he was doing," Felix insisted.

"I said I've got it."

He stood up and went toe to toe with Felix. The man was dangerous, a mix of drug-fueled mania and the righteous indignation of a person no one had ever stopped. Least of all his doting father, who thought the sun rose and fell on his precious twins.

Felix didn't have any subtlety in his expressions; he either hated or didn't, and there was a venomous hate in his eyes right now.

"Back. The Fuck. Off," Felix ordered. He was vibrating with rage, and his expression was becoming more unfocused as the red heat of temper climbed from his dark heart.

Deacon could play this two ways. He could kill Felix, close his hands around that bastard's neck and squeeze until he was dead, expose his cover, get himself killed. Or he could play his damn part and play it well.

Forcing himself to relax, he stepped back and tilted his head in deference. "He's all yours," he said.

Felix wrinkled his nose, then grinned. "Too fucking right," he said.

"I'll tell your dad you'll be down in a minute," Deacon said, deceptively quiet, and he saw the indecision on Felix's face. Felix never went against his dad, probably because he actually respected the old man.

Felix kicked out at Rafe one last time.

"I'm not wasting my time on him." He poked Deacon in the chest, and Deacon had to fight the instinct to snap his hand back and break every bone in his fingers. "You find out what he was doing."

"Let's go," Chumo said, and backed away from the situation.

Felix cursed, and Deacon steeled himself for Felix to get in one more kick or punch. He didn't, but he hadn't finished with the words.

"I mean it – find out what the little fairy was doing," he ordered.

Deacon fought the very strong instinct to beat Rafe to a pulp, and stayed in character.

"On it," he agreed.

"Fucker was going through—"

"I've got this," Deacon interrupted.

"Sir," Felix added.

"I've got this, sir," Deacon replied dutifully.

That seemed to be enough to have Felix stalking away, Chumo falling into his normal position a few steps behind. Now, Deacon had time to get Rafe to understand how much shit he was in.

Only when he was sure they had gone did he crouch down by Rafe.

"Get up," he said, softening his tone a little, and nudged at one of Rafe's hands with his own.

"Go 'way," Rafe muttered. It was a start – at least he was talking.

"Get up, Rafe," Deacon said, and nudged him again.

Rafe scrambled away in a sudden uncoordinated move and used the wall to stand. For a while he kept his eyes shut, and he swayed in a dangerous manner. Deacon held out a hand to steady him, but it was as if Rafe knew what Deacon was doing, and he took a step back, his foot stepping awkwardly on a textbook. He windmilled his arms to stay upright, his eyes opening abruptly.

This time Deacon got hold of him, gripping his shirt and then his arm, yanking him upright, then supporting him until he got his bearings. Only as soon as that happened, Rafe pulled his arm free and went into a crouch to pick up his books and stationery and all the loose notebooks. Deacon stooped to help, but Rafe let out this small noise that was equal parts pain and anger, and Deacon backed off. He knew a cornered, wounded animal when he saw one. Rafe stuffed everything in his bag and turned to leave, Deacon following.

"What?" Rafe snapped, and spun on his heel. He was scarlet – with temper, or embarrassment, or pain, Deacon couldn't tell.

"Are you okay?"

"I'm fine."

Rafe didn't sound *fine*; he sounded as though he was just about to crack in half.

Deacon shrugged as if the way Rafe was standing and looking at him didn't have a single iota of effect on him. "I need to find out what happened."

Rafe, all bristling temper, stepped up into Deacon's space; a good six inches shorter than him, he had to crane his head back to look up at him, and there was fire in his eyes.

"One of my cousins is a psycho, and the other cousin is a sycophantic asshole, and I'm going to my room to revise." Embarrassment was abruptly lost in pure anger.

He walked off again, and Deacon was right on his heels, only this time Rafe didn't stop him or talk to him, only let himself into his room, then waited for Deacon to follow him.

"Get on with it," he said dispassionately, as if he was expecting something from Deacon. A beating, or hateful words.

"Rafe—"

"Fuck you, Deacon – you're no better than they are."

"That's bullshit," Deacon snapped, then realized what he'd done. Was he really going to blow everything by exposing the true Deacon, the one who had kissed Rafe the night before?

This was nothing like it had been in the darkness at the side of the lake; this was Rafe back in his hard shell.

Deacon shut the door behind him, and only then did a flicker of fear pass over Rafe's face. He clutched his bag to his chest, solid armor against whatever Deacon could do to him.

"I'm not going to hurt you," Deacon murmured.

"I don't believe you," Rafe snapped. "I've seen you try it all now."

"What do you mean?"

"Hurting me, kissing me, confusing me – I'm not falling for any of it."

Deacon didn't know where to start with any of that, and in the end he fell back to being as honest as he could.

"Rafe, you've got to stop doing whatever it is you're doing."

Rafe stiffened and tilted his chin in defiance. Deacon could see the moment Rafe's shields came up and the lying began.

"I don't know what you mean," he said with fake confidence.

Deacon sighed. Rafe was a pretty poor liar. Unlike his cousin, Felix, every expression Rafe felt was telegraphed on his face. That and the fact that he was gorgeous and sensitive and needed Deacon in his life was what had led to them kissing the night before.

"Why were you in the office?" Deacon pressed. "Just give me some kind of credible reason here."

He needed to pass something on to the family. Security was his job, and that included coming up with a plausible reason why Rafe had been rooting around his uncle's office. He had to stay undercover long enough to get this job done, and that started with balancing all the truths and lies that lay between him and Rafe.

Rafe tipped his chin again and clenched his fists at his sides, looking every inch the scrappy fighter he needed to be to survive this poisonous family. "I was looking for a damn stapler," he said.

"Don't lie to me, please." Deacon didn't have to be an expert in body language to see the tightening of Rafe's jaw or the way he couldn't quite meet Deacon's eyes.

Deacon wanted to shake the idiot. All Rafe had to do was get through his finals, and he could get out of this place. He shouldn't be here in this place.

"You lie to me," Rafe said.

And he wasn't wrong. Deacon wanted to tell Rafe that he was there to take the Martinez family apart from the inside. He wanted to blow the cover that had taken two years to create. He wanted to haul Rafe into his arms and kiss him and promise him he would do anything to keep him safe. He couldn't do any of that.

He'd been guarding Rafe for three weeks now, and every single day the younger man had pulled at him in ways he'd never understood before. Deacon wasn't stupid; he knew he was attracted to Rafe, to his tenacity, his bravery, and his goddamn stubbornness that one day could get him killed.

"I want you to leave," he said, not adding an explanation. It was a familiar refrain; he'd said the same thing the night before, just before he'd hauled Rafe in and kissed him.

"No," Rafe whispered. "I won't leave."

"I can't keep you safe—"

"I'm not asking you to."

"Rafe, please."

"No."

Deacon steeled himself to try a different direction, slipping back into the hard-man persona that was getting more impossible to find each day he was around Rafe.

"Sit down," he ordered.

Rafe stared at him mutinously for a moment, then the fight left him and, with his bag still huddled close to him, he sat on the edge of his bed. Deacon moved closer and they began a short but terrier-like battle over the bag. Deacon finally got it away from him and placed it gently on the bed next to him. Then he reached out and pressed a hand under Rafe's chin, raising his face and examining the cut where his teeth had torn into his soft lips.

There was the smudge of red near his eye, and that would likely bruise as well. He softened at the hurt he could see there. Underneath the not very professional intrigue he had going on, Rafe was a quiet guy, happy to sit in the restaurant when it was empty and study. He had glasses he pushed up his nose when they had a tendency to slip down, and long, layered hair that hung around his face, giving him a gentle appearance. Startling green eyes were framed with long lashes and he had this way of staring at Deacon when he thought Deacon wasn't watching.

"Your face," Deacon murmured, and using his other hand he brushed away Rafe's hair. This was dangerous; this was caring about someone he had no right to care about.

But Rafe didn't react to the times Felix intimidated him or bullied him; he closed his eyes and let everything wash over him. He never called out, he never argued, and Felix was close to losing his shit with Rafe; any idiot could see that. Felix was a typical bully. He wanted Rafe crying and on his knees.

Deacon was older than Rafe, and even as he looked up at him with soft eyes, Deacon could see the man he would become.

"I thought you were different," Rafe murmured, his voice breaking, so much emotion dripping from every syllable. "Last night, when you kissed me…"

"That shouldn't have happened," Deacon interjected before Rafe could continue.

Rafe raised his hand and settled it over Deacon's. "You don't belong here," he said, his tone questioning. "You're not the same as them."

Deacon wavered, leaned closer, and for a second he was going to kiss Rafe, just as they had in the dark. One kiss and he'd lost his fucking mind. Training kicked him back into line, and he leaned back, seeing the flash of hurt in Rafe's eyes.

"Your dad wouldn't want you hurt like this," Deacon murmured.

"You didn't know my dad," Rafe said sadly. "You wouldn't know what he wanted for me."

"I know his son well enough."

Rafe's breath hitched. "You don't. You can't really know me, not yet."

"Go back to college, get your degree, be the best person you can be."

Jeez, now he was waxing lyrical. But Rafe only had one semester left until graduation in pre-law, finishing the credits online, and then he'd go on to law school as he was supposed to and he'd make a markedly different impact on the world than Deacon did. Rafe would be pure innocence, fighting for the little guy, making things right, and Deacon would continue to be on the blunt end of taking down the bad guys.

Rafe looked at him, and his eyes glittered brightly with emotion. "Maybe *you* could be the one who makes me the best person I can be."

God, Rafe was going to kill him talking like that.

"You don't know what you're talking about," Deacon said, his tone hard. The years that separated them had been hard, and he was left with all kinds of scars on his skin and even darker marks on his soul. Yet Rafe looked at him as if he saw something other than his scruffy beard and his messy blond hair. He'd been looked at before, times when he guessed people had judged him and found him wanting, but that was part of his job. Rafe, on the other hand, stared at him as though he couldn't get a real handle on what Deacon was.

And that was dangerous, to Rafe, but most of all to Deacon.

Rafe circled his wrist, but Deacon couldn't guess if he was going to push him away or hold him still. His heart was sore; he hated undercover when innocent people were getting hurt, but this was bigger than Rafe. Bigger than anyone could know.

"Deacon?" Rafe murmured.

"What?" He was being lulled, pulled in by Rafe's hesitant use of his name. He was leaning in, down, and Rafe tugged on his hand, rising to his feet. The kiss was so close that Deacon could feel it.

Fuck. He could taste it.

"Deacon…" This time there was no question on Rafe's lips, and it was that which thrust Deacon back into the here and now.

He snapped back into being the tough guy, the bad one who could physically wound Rafe.

"Where do you hurt?" he asked, and cleared his throat at how gruff he sounded to his own ears.

"Nowhere," Rafe said, and he moved his chin away from Deacon's touch. "Why didn't you kiss me?"

"Get some salve on that lip."

"Shit, Deacon."

"No talking. I don't know why you think I would want to kiss you again, kid. Stay away from Felix."

Rafe crossed his arms over his chest, much as he'd used his bag defensively.

"Get out of my room."

Deacon held himself rigid and met Rafe's hardening gaze. "That was my plan," he said dryly.

Only outside the door did he realize how close he'd come to fucking everything up. Felix was making his way up the long corridor, intent in his walk. Likely he was on his way to check up on the situation. Deacon made a show of touching the knuckles of his right hand, and saw Felix glance down at them, a feral gleam in his eye.

Felix came to a stop next to him. "You warmed him up for me—"

"You're not touching him," Deacon interrupted, and his cover slipped into place. "Your dad was explicit in his instructions that the kid was to be watched and that was it."

"Then he shouldn't be in Dad's office."

"He was looking for a stapler."

"And you fell for that?"

"I don't give a shit what he was doing. I have my orders, and if he steps out of line, then it will be me who does the beating."

"You work for me—"

"No, sir, I don't. I work for your dad."

There was an epic staredown. At least it would have been epic had Felix not started muttering to himself and walked away after the first few seconds. There was something seriously wrong with this man that wanted to rail on Rafe at a moment's notice. Something evil in Felix's eyes that screamed of insanity. It wouldn't be the first time Deacon had seen that level of craziness in the kind of people he got involved with, and it likely wouldn't be the last.

All he could do now was hope that, at least for the rest of the day, Rafe stayed in his room where he would be safe, and Deacon had successfully neutralized Felix.

He'd known this gig wasn't going to be easy, but he'd never expected to feel affection for one of the people he'd been sent to watch.

"I have a bad feeling about this," he muttered to the empty corridor.

A really bad feeling.

CHAPTER 3

Rafe was mortified on so many levels. He'd tried to flirt with Deacon, and after last night's kiss he'd wanted more.

But he was fucking it all up. He needed to take a step back and be clever about this.

What if Felix had found Rafe moments earlier? What if Felix had found the photos that Rafe had taken, or beaten him unconscious for whatever reason his asshole cousin chose?

Fucking stupid. Rafe berated himself for that until he'd finally processed the fact that he'd nearly fucked everything up, then moved swiftly on to the shame and embarrassment of what had happened next. Deacon had found him, which was bad enough, but then he'd nearly kissed the man again. The thug his uncle had hired to keep the peace, and do whatever else it was discreet security did for an outwardly respectable company. Deacon probably killed people, or at least beat them worse than Felix ever could.

But god, how Rafe wanted to kiss him again. Deacon was danger and fire and so fucking sexy it made Rafe mad with the need of it.

On top of that, Rafe had to pretend he understood and noticed nothing, had to act as if he was thick as shit and twice as stupid. He had to look Uncle Arlo in the eyes and say that security was clearly an okay thing, and wasn't it good that he had someone to keep the family safe.

Safe from voters, or the guy on the corner who used to stand and shout up at the open office window. The same guy who had conveniently vanished just under three weeks ago. Had Deacon been tasked with killing the short, skinny man who'd shouted that the Martinez bastard would pay

Pay for what?

Rafe had actually stood waiting to talk to the guy, but had never got the chance. Because the unnamed man had vanished. No one knew where he'd gone, or even who he was, despite Rafe's discreet inquiries. Another chance lost.

But seriously, what kind of alderman needs personal security?

Locking his door, he pulled out his phone and scrolled to the last four photos. Maps on his Uncle's wall, real estate parcels of land along with zoning details and a list of numbers to one side. Before anyone tried to get in by breaking down his door, which he wouldn't put past his psycho cousin, he uploaded the photos to his remote file service and watched the bar as it crept to one hundred percent. When they were gone, he deleted the pictures on his phone and took random photos of his textbooks instead. He had no idea if the deleted images were still up in the cloud connected to his name. He hoped to hell not – he thought he'd turned off all the options he needed to, but he wasn't a technical expert, and had just followed security advice on websites he'd searched for on Google.

Fuck it; he would prove that Arlo had been the one who'd killed his father, or at least ordered the hit-and-run that had left Héctor Ramirez dead at sixty-four. Grief curled inside him again, and all the energy left his body.

He pressed fingers to his split lip and winced at the pain, which at least grounded him and let him think about why he was even there. The ache from the two punches to the gut was a dull pain, and he pulled up his knees, which eased the tightness in his belly.

Rafe was frustrated; he had photos of maps, but what did any of it mean? According to his dad, the construction business was a front for much more sinister things. That that was where the bodies were buried. But had his dad meant that literally or figuratively?

Rafe wanted action. He wanted Arlo to admit the accident that had taken his father had in fact been no accident at all.

He wanted Arlo to confess.

Tears pricked his eyes and, unbidden, his thought process worked from his dad and the pain in his heart, onto the ache in his gut and the injustice of what had happened with Felix, and then right on through to Deacon.

Hazel-eyed, blond-haired Deacon, who stood inches taller than him, broader than him, who carried a gun and scars on those parts of his body that Rafe had seen.

Deacon was everything his dad had warned him against; rough, nasty, a man who thought and dealt with ingrained violence, a man with a gun. A bad guy.

But there was something in his eyes – concern, a moment before the mask dropped when Deacon looked at him differently. Or was Rafe just looking for things that weren't there?

"I don't know why he would," Rafe muttered to no one. He was trapped here, he wanted to be here, he couldn't escape from this family, but he didn't want to. This whole thing was a mess.

A shower helped with the general aches, and he downed some Tylenol with a bottle of water before gathering up his last project before finals. The irony of the question from his philosophy class didn't escape him: "Is it objectionably paradoxical to claim it is wrong to kill someone to prevent two other people from being killed?"

Would it have been wrong to take a gun and shoot Arlo to prevent him from hurting Rafe's father? Would it be wrong to shoot Felix before he went out and killed someone?

Rafe knew he had to look at this objectively, but he was tired. Coffee was the answer, and he glanced at his watch. Three twenty-four p.m. The restaurant the family owned wouldn't be alive and kicking for another two hours – plenty of time to set up at one of the back tables, work on this question with books out around him, and help himself to coffee from the main machine down there. He gathered up what he needed and cautiously unlocked and opened his door. No sign of Felix, but he knew he'd have Deacon on his tail as soon as he left the room.

He wasn't wrong. Deacon fell into step with him as soon he reached the top of the stairs.

"I don't get it," he said, shifting the weight of the bag on his shoulder and wincing at the twinge of pain in his back. Felix had gotten in a good kick.

"What?" Deacon asked as they reached the bottom of the stairs and turned left for the restaurant.

He had so many questions, about the kiss in the dark, about the vulnerability he sometimes thought he saw in

Deacon. But at this point in time only one thing worried him.

"Why do you have to guard me?"

But Deacon didn't answer. He just went with the normal routine; Rafe at the table studying, and him sitting by the door.

Watching.

CHAPTER 4

Deacon was slowly losing his mind.

"And?"

The question from his partner, out there watching the house, hung waiting to be answered. Deacon wished to hell he had an answer for Evie that would get him out of this city and back home to New York. Six months was long enough, and he'd started to forget what his own place looked like. What did Evie want him to say? That Arlo had made a deal with some shady nebulous bad guys and he had evidence of it? Or that he'd seen one of Arlo's sons do something bad enough they deserved to be arrested? Because fuck if either of those things had happened. Apart from baiting Rafe, there was nothing he could find that would lead to any kind of conviction. Beating Rafe wasn't going to get the charge he wanted. Of course, when he'd arrived here, he'd expected to be pulled into the fold, but then he realized he'd been called in to babysit Arlo's nephew.

Arlo's sexy, confusing, brilliant young nephew.

"Need more time," he typed into the encrypted software, and pressed send. The word sent and vanished like it had never been there.

"Shit," came the flashing reply, which disappeared instantly.

Shit was exactly right. There was a damn good reason why he had nothing to report, and that reason was sitting at another table in the restaurant, papers spread around him in careful piles. Rafe Ramirez, with his clear green eyes and his open smile, was the one thing that Deacon was not losing sight of.

For the wrong reasons altogether.

So he lied. Right there and then, he told Evie the biggest pile of shit. Bryan had wanted to talk to him – maybe that would be something new to follow up on.

"New lead," he typed, keeping the message short. Not that anyone would see him typing, or be able to read it. Certainly not Rafe, with his head in his books and with the whole length of the restaurant between them. Deacon was by the door, between him and the exit, watching carefully, and he'd been treated to Rafe turning and looking at him with a confused expression on his face at least three times. The last time had morphed into a hesitant smile, and Deacon had had to lower his gaze. That damn kiss was like a landmine between them, waiting to explode.

He was clearly losing his mind here if a smile and the memory of a kiss could pull his focus from this case. Rafe's uncle was the target, and Deacon had to focus on that. Of course, it didn't help that being hired by Arlo had been the easy part; following him was impossible when he'd been handed babysitting duty instead.

"More?" The message appeared, and Deacon had to think before he remembered the question was about a missing person. The disappearance was exactly why his section had been called in to handle this case. When a body had turned up a year ago, it had become Deacon's case. Now he was so mired in the family to get an in with them that he was clearly losing all perspective.

The only thing that worried him was the case of a missing person. Bryan, one of the younger guys here, had been at the house yesterday. Deacon had found him, looking fucking terrified, in the wine cellar and nearly broken cover to talk to Bryan. Instead he'd added Bryan to the list of people he was looking out for. He was some distant cousin, but this morning he'd been gone. Deacon wanted to think he'd run, but Felix had been strutting this morning, like the cat who'd drunk the cream, and that didn't bode well. So that was a case. Right?

"Soon," he typed and sent, then shut down the secure connection when he saw Rafe stand up and stretch tall, his T-shirt riding up. He was shorter than Deacon, slim, a little gangly, as if he hadn't grown into his body yet, even at twenty-three. He kept fit running on the elliptical in the small gym in the basement, never did weights. He was young, fit and toned, and Deacon couldn't help but stare.

Because Deacon was a fucking idiot who, instead of keeping his head in the case, was focusing on the wrong thing.

Only they'd kissed; they'd moved closer and Deacon had been *this close* to kissing Rafe again. And he was confused.

He pocketed his cell and caught Rafe miming drinking from a cup looking right at him. He nodded, and a few minutes later, after Rafe had played with the dials on the huge espresso machine that was front and center of Milo's, he placed a coffee in front of Deacon.

"I'm nearly done," he said, but there was no hint of a smile now. "I'm really sorry my uncle thinks you need to babysit me."

"Don't be," Deacon said.

"I still don't get why I need it."

Deacon kept his expression neutral, hearing the slight lift at the end of that statement, which made it sound like a question. No way was he opening that can of worms by entering into a discussion of what Rafe's uncle was or wasn't.

So instead he focused on the pretty in front of him. He actually had shower fantasies featuring Rafe in all kinds of positions, but he would never act on them, even if he wanted to. God knew what it was about Rafe that had him salivating at the thought of a taste. Was it the absolute innocence in a man so entwined in the mess that was Arlo and his sons? Or was it just the way he smiled? Rafe was trying for a small smile now, but clearly his split lip hurt, as he winced and pressed a finger there, looking down at it to check for blood.

Temper spiked inside Deacon, but he couldn't blow his cover by getting all serious over one cousin *teasing* another. Because teasing was what Arlo had called it when Deacon had reported what had happened. Asshole.

Fuck, he felt so protective of Rafe.

In another world, Deacon would have made his move, but this was not that world; this was drugs and despair and a hundred other sick things that made his stomach churn and that Rafe knew nothing about. Or at least Deacon hoped he didn't. He was having to trust his gut that Rafe was entirely innocent.

Except how could Rafe not know the man his uncle was? He had to know.

"Deacon?"

Deacon looked up from contemplating the world in his coffee, and realized that Rafe hadn't moved.

"Yes kid?"

Rafe frowned. "Stop calling me that," he said without heat. "I'm twenty-three, for fuck's sake," he tagged on to the end, as though Deacon might not know that. "I'm a fucking adult, and I hate the way people think that just because I look young, I can't be anything other than a kid. You fucking kissed me, so fuck you for calling me a kid."

Deacon looked back down at his coffee. "I won't call you that again," he murmured.

"Shit. Sorry," Rafe said, defeated, and sat in the chair opposite him. "I guess you're not wrong."

That wasn't what Deacon needed at this point in time. He needed Rafe to go back to his studying and stop getting all up in Deacon's space.

"Because you're, what, thirty? You still see me as a kid," Rafe said, resting his chin on his hands and staring Deacon down.

Deacon shifted on his chair a little. No, what he saw was a man who had pinned his sights on getting Deacon to chat as if they were close or something. And hell, to kiss him.

Why, Deacon didn't know. He was twelve years older than Rafe, and he had a lifetime of mess in his fucked-up head.

"Thirty-five. And yeah, you are still a kid in my eyes," Deacon said simply, and sipped the caffeine that would keep him alert for the rest of Rafe's study session.

Unfortunately, Rafe wasn't letting things go.

"I'm twenty-three. I drink, I have sex…" He trailed off and did this thing with his mouth that was half irritated and half the sexiest thing Deacon had ever seen. And he was leaning forward again, and the scent of him – a combination of shower gel and Rafe – was getting to him. Deliberately, he sat way back in his chair. Seemed like Rafe had forgotten to be angry with Deacon for pulling away.

So he decided to shut this down. He leaned forward as if he wanted to say something quiet, and Rafe moved closer, his eyes widening.

"Go back and study," Deacon half whispered, then quirked an eyebrow.

Rafe sat back with a huff and began to say something, but was interrupted when the door slammed open.

"Fairy taking up your time?" Felix's harsh, nasal voice resonated in the quiet restaurant.

Rafe, with his back to Felix, closed his eyes briefly, and Deacon wished at that moment that he could reach over and reassure Rafe that Felix was a complete asshole who was really close to spending time in jail.

But he couldn't.

His cover wasn't a caring-is-sharing kind of guy – his role was the enforcer, and it was one that was selling tickets in this family, with everyone buying in. Well, all except for Rafe, who looked at him with confusion rather than fear or respect.

"Fuck," Rafe bit out under his breath. He rose from his seat and went back to his table.

Felix walked past him, flicking at the Dodgers cap that covered his unruly brown hair. Its layers had a tendency to curl in the damp, stormy heat of a Californian summer afternoon, something that Deacon should not be noticing.

Rafe gave Felix the finger, and Felix tapped the back of his head a little harder than necessary. Why the hell was Rafe provoking him?

God, it would be so good when Deacon had enough to get Felix behind bars.

And Chumo, who came in after his brother, forever his twin's shadow. He was dressed to the nines in a sharp suit, his hands in fists at his sides. He looked pissed, and Deacon tensed. He'd never seen Chumo angry before – quietly, coldly focused, but never cross over anything.

"You're an asshole, Felix." He shoved his brother. "You left me standing with her."

Felix shoved back, only he shoved harder, sending Chumo right into Rafe's table.

Deacon stood up. There was no way he was letting Rafe get in the middle of some sibling squabble. But it ended as soon as it began, with Felix – bigger, stronger – pinning his twin and putting his weight behind the move.

"Get off me," Chumo snapped. He shoved back, and Felix let him go, holding his hands up and grinning.

"She was hot for some prime Martinez cock," Felix said, and held out a fist, which Chumo bumped.

"Well, she's getting it," Chumo said, shaking off his brother and suddenly grinning. "We're hooking up after dinner."

They bumped fists again. "Way to go, bro," Felix said.

Then they moved away, up the stairs to the offices that ran the full length of the building. Deacon considered going over to see if Rafe was okay, but that wasn't part of his job. Rafe did look over at him, but Deacon pretended to have a need to stare at the candle in the middle of the table. Not so much a coward, but a man absolutely focused on his job.

He sat back in his chair after a while, looking at Rafe's back, at the curls under his cap, and hoped to hell that Rafe got out of this venomous mess before he became like his cousins. Deacon had actually raised this with his handler, but all he'd got in response was an instruction to wait things out. Rafe had only been there a few weeks, but the contagion in the place would get into his blood, and he could change.

Of course, given his last name and his family, there wasn't any way in hell Rafe was getting out of living there with a clean record, or even alive. Not unless Deacon could be a hundred percent sure that Rafe wasn't wholly or partly involved with his uncle and cousins' business. The department was looking at Rafe as part of what was happening here, and all Deacon could do was hope that he could prove otherwise.

And looking at the young man with the smile and the gorgeous green eyes, Deacon knew that if Rafe *was* involved, it was a tragic waste.

And he definitely shouldn't have kissed him.

Dinner was the same rowdy affair it always was. Arlo, the patriarch of the family, surrounded himself with those he considered *familia*, even those with a nebulous connection. Those with the closest ties sat near Arlo, with the hangers-on at the end of the long pine table. The ones at the end were third cousins, or with some link to Cuba, which made them acceptable in Arlo's eyes.

Deacon took his place, leaning against the door. He didn't eat with the family; his place was to look menacing and to keep an eye on Rafe. Arlo's words, not his. Arlo sat at the head of the table, his wife on his left-hand side. A pinched woman, she never really looked as if she wanted to be there, and wasn't quick to speak on any subject, a fact that seemed to suit Arlo down to the ground. The twins were on the other side, with Felix next to his dad. Deacon had quickly assessed that Felix was the dominant twin, Chumo often showing his belly in arguments. Felix was definitely the favored son.

And then next to his aunt, right opposite Chumo, sat Rafe. He looked uncomfortable sitting there, his gaze firmly fixed on his plate, his shoulders hunched, and he was never the first to make conversation.

"Saw what was left of that homo kid at the ring," Felix said, making sure his voice was loud enough for everyone to take notice. Which of course everyone did. The family owned a boxing club, and Felix loved nothing more than beating on people smaller than him. Fuck knew why the place hadn't been shut down yet. "They had to take his sparkly ass out on a stretcher."

Rafe didn't look up from his plate; he had to know as well as everyone else at the table exactly where this was going. Rafe had not been backward in telling his new family that he was gay. It was as much a part of him as his eyes, or his ability to sketch cartoon characters in the sides of his course notebooks. Felix was sometimes gleeful in his stories about how he dealt with "the queers". He was dangerous.

"Enough, Felix," Arlo said, but his voice wasn't strident as it usually was when he told people what to do. No, it was sly and slimy, and Deacon wanted to punch the man in the head. Of course, he'd have to settle for seeing Arlo behind bars, but he would freaking enjoy it if he got to punch him on the way in.

"Sorry, Dad," Felix said, but continued anyway. "I said they shouldn't let him in the ring – knew he'd get pummeled by the next guy after I was done with him. Took two men to hold him still for the beating, though – he had fucking fancy footwork when he tried running."

"Language," Arlo admonished.

"So they called the paramedics, and it didn't look good. Hell, maybe the next guy beat some straight into him."

Rafe looked up at that, his eyes glowing with a combination of anger and hatred, and Deacon saw the moment Felix knew he'd succeeded in hitting his mark.

"Seems to me," Felix said, silky smooth, "you shouldn't ever take up boxing, Rafe, being a bit *delicate* an' all."

Felix laughed at his joke, and half the table did as well, including Arlo.

"Not built for boxing," Chumo pointed out, which made more people laugh.

Rafe said nothing, just as he never said anything, because there was no freaking point.

Dinner pretty much went downhill from there, and Rafe excused himself as soon as dessert was done. Arlo looked at Deacon pointedly and inclined his head slightly, and with a returning nod Deacon left the dining room and followed Rafe. He didn't want to – he wanted to be in the room where the action was, where he'd possibly overhear enough to take the entire Martinez family down. Rafe included, if needed be. He just had to trust that the bugs he'd personally installed over the last few weeks were actually transmitting as they should.

"You don't need to follow me," Rafe snapped when Deacon caught up with him.

He was at a T-junction in the long corridor. To the left were the bedrooms, to the right were the offices that were permanently locked. Deacon had seen the body language in Rafe that had shouted he'd been going right and had changed his mind at the last moment.

"Just looking out for you," Deacon said.

Rafe muttered something under his breath that sounded suspiciously like "asshole" and "sexy", but he couldn't quite hear.

"Stalking me, you mean," he added, and took the stairs to his room, bypassing it and climbing the next flight to the roof. He held the door open for Deacon as he knew Deacon would be right on his tail.

They exited onto the roof. It was nothing special; a flat space with various ducts and a large metal shed with its doors hanging off. Deacon knew every inch of this rooftop, including the perfect point from which to jump if he needed to get to the next building, where his handler sat monitoring everything Deacon was in the middle of.

He also knew that this was Rafe's quiet place. In the three weeks Deacon had been watching Rafe, he'd inevitably gravitated to the far corner with views over the river, and he would push his hands into his pockets and simply stare out over the water.

"Why do you do it?" he asked as he stared forward. "Work for my uncle?" He turned to face Deacon, and his expression was a picture of openness; he wanted to know what it took for a man to be a gun for hire, a pseudo bodyguard, the heavy guy to do what needed to be done. How much of what his uncle had going on was known to Rafe? Deacon didn't have an answer, because even though he had a solid backstory, part of him just didn't want to lie to Rafe. There was too much confusion between them as it was.

So he said nothing at all.

"I guess you can't say anything, eh?" Rafe concluded, and turned back to the water. "I just need you to leave me alone."

Deacon stepped closer to look at the view that kept Rafe enthralled. This was prime real estate in this town, on a slight hill. Built in the thirties it was solid stone, with manicured gardens winding past outbuildings down to the endlessly deep lake. From here you could see the end of the small jetty, and the water was flat and gray in the darkening evening.

"I'm paid to look out for you," Deacon reminded Rafe. "Your uncle worries about you."

Rafe huffed a laugh. "Cut the crap," he said harshly, the laugh turning into a barely concealed snarl. "You know you're lying." He turned abruptly and stepped right into Deacon's space, shoving at him, hard. "You're all wrong. You don't fit here any more than I do," he added, and shoved again.

Deacon's chest tightened. That sounded a lot like an accusation. He grasped Rafe's hand and pushed him away, acutely aware that if Rafe came too close he'd say fuck it and drag him in for a kiss.

Rafe yelped at the same time Deacon realized he was holding Rafe's hand way too tight. Deacon immediately let go, which made Rafe stumble, which led to Deacon holding him way too close to stop him from hitting the ground. They were alone up here. He was playing a role. His team wouldn't care; they'd expect him to use every avenue he had to dig into what was happening here, and if that included kissing the nephew who didn't quite fit into the family, then they would understand that. It wouldn't be the first skin job he'd undertaken and it wouldn't be the last.

But what if someone came onto the roof?

No one comes out here except Rafe.

What if Felix decided to track Rafe down?

Felix is with his father, which is where I should be; right at Arlo's side.

He'd run out of excuses, and Rafe was looking up at him, gripping his shirt, with naked need in his eyes.

And Deacon couldn't help himself.

One more kiss wouldn't be wrong. Right?

But when their lips met, it became long, drawn out, a battle of wills on his part, a greedy, breath-stealing grab of a kiss from Rafe. They didn't move, wrapped around each other in the dark, kissing as though they were in another place, and it was another time, and it was okay for them to be doing this.

He didn't know why they pulled apart; he thought it must have been him, but he wasn't sure. He wanted another taste, but there was too much distance between them and he wasn't ready to tug Rafe back.

"Who are you really?" Rafe asked, his fingers touching his lips.

God, he wanted to tell Rafe so badly, wanted to trust Rafe didn't know anything about his uncle, or the kind of criminal activities that were paying for the remainder of Rafe's education.

He couldn't.

Deacon had a best friend, a former marine and the man next door to whom he'd grown up, Mackenzie Jackson. He'd always said that Deacon was an enigma.

When they'd gotten drunk last, too many years ago to mention, kids who didn't know better, Mac had summed Deacon up in three words: "marshmallow hard-man". Which, of course, had led to an in-depth discussion about *Ghostbusters*.

Ultimately, he never had fully asked Mac what he meant, but standing here looking at Rafe, he had an idea. He'd been undercover on this case for nearly a year in various lowly positions – grunt work and the like – and he was standing here nearly blowing all that hard work. He'd moved slowly into the circles that would catch Arlo Martinez's attention, and when he'd finally got a way in, he'd known he was so close to getting Arlo behind bars.

He couldn't lose sight of that now in the face of a man too young for him with innocence in eyes that sometimes flashed fire.

"We need to go back in," Deacon said, and turned to go inside.

At first he thought Rafe might argue, but then he heard footsteps behind him. He saw Rafe to his room, heard the door lock, and after a while he went back downstairs. His room was next to Rafe's, and unknown to the younger man, his uncle had it bugged with both audio and video feeds. Deacon could see Rafe there, lying on his stomach on his bed, his arms crossed under a pillow. There was nothing creepier than having this window into Rafe's world.

He dozed, woken by the soft alarm that warned him Rafe had left his room. A quick glance at the clock, and it was a little after three a.m. The house was quiet, and Deacon eased out of his door. The place was big enough that it was a rabbit warren of stairs and corridors and small rooms, but Deacon instinctively knew that Rafe was heading right back to the office.

Idiot.

He would catch up with him, get him back to his room, and hell, maybe he should be honest about what he was doing here…but he was too late.

Rounding the corner, he came across a tableau that made his heart stop.

Rafe on his knees, and Felix with a gun to his temple, the door to the office wide open behind them. Felix looked up at Deacon. He looked unfocused in the light spilling into the hallway, as if he was high, and his mouth was set in a line.

"I'm gonna kill him," he said, and the gun shook a little right against Rafe's skin.

"Felix—"

"I'm gonna fucking kill the son of a bitch."

CHAPTER 5

Rafe closed his eyes, the feel of cold metal on his skin enough to make him think this was where it all ended.

He'd seen Deacon arrive, seen the horror in his expression. But it wasn't like he was leaping to Rafe's rescue.

Of all the shit to happen, he had to jimmy the lock and walk in on Felix snorting cocaine off the large oak desk, his pants around his thighs and porn on the computer.

He'd attempted to back out, but he'd stumbled on the door jamb, and Chumo had been there. He'd moved so fast, and Felix had joined him, grabbing at any part of Rafe, waving a gun.

"On your fucking knees," Felix had ordered, and for a moment – a brief, panicked moment – Rafe had imagined that Felix wanted him to suck him off, his cock hanging out, his jeans snagged on his thighs. But no, as Felix yanked at the denim, the gun pointing at his face, Rafe realized this wasn't about sex – this was about death.

"Chumo? What happened?"

"Not my problem," Chumo muttered, and Rafe heard him move away.

"What the fuck, Felix?" Deacon asked loudly.

"Caught the fairy breaking into Dad's office," Felix shouted, and pressed the gun so hard against Rafe's head that he was leaning on the wall, the gun holding him in place. He hadn't wanted things to go this way. He'd wanted to find the evidence that Arlo had killed his dad;

he'd wanted his day in court, watching Arlo answer for a hundred crimes.

But it seemed he was going to die, and he kept his eyes tightly closed.

"Give me the fucking gun," Deacon ordered. "We don't do shit this way."

The gun moved, but clearly Felix hadn't passed it to Deacon, because it was still hard and heavy against his skin. Then it moved away from him.

"Don't fucking point it at me," Deacon snarled, then there was a scuffle and a thud.

Still Rafe didn't open his eyes.

The commotion had drawn an audience; his cousin's voice, his uncle's, and then the gentlest of touches to his chin.

"Look at me, Rafe," Uncle Arlo said, and finally Rafe opened his eyes. "What were you doing?"

Deacon was there, staring down at him, his arms crossed over his chest, Felix's gun in his hand. There was no smile, no connection, and he looked deadly.

"Stand up," Arlo ordered, and gestured for Deacon to help him, which Deacon did, yanking him into a standing position but holding him steady. "Talk to me," Arlo began. "I took you in, in memory of my brother—"

"You killed him," Rafe snapped. He wasn't living past tonight; in his heart, he knew that.

Arlo shook his head, as if he was humoring Rafe, then his grip on reality appeared to loosen, and he went from benign uncle to madman. He closed his hands around Rafe's throat, loosely at first and then tighter.

"My sister was a whore to marry that man," he snarled, spitting the last word into Rafe's face. "He was a traitor. I'm ashamed of you," Arlo shouted. "You have my blood, but you are nothing but a waste of skin. How could God bring a man like your father into my life to betray me?"

"You're fucked," Rafe shouted. "Any god you pray to won't forgive you for what you do."

Arlo shook him, and Deacon loosened his hold on Rafe's arm.

"You whoreson," Arlo added with a shove.

Rafe wasn't backing down. "I've heard stories of what happened to my mom. Dad told me she didn't die in a car accident, that she'd been beaten to death. You did that," Rafe shouted at his uncle over the chokehold. He was aware that the game he was playing was a dangerous one, but what had happened to his mom had been a horror he could only imagine, and his dad's dying words had damned Arlo to hell.

Arlo was a murderer, and Rafe's parents had both died by his hand. He was sure of it. There was no way he was leaving this Earth without taking down Arlo and his sons.

This family had black blood.

"You don't know what you're talking about," Arlo snapped, and shook him. Rafe thought he saw Deacon move a little, but he must have imagined it, because Deacon wasn't doing anything.

"Take him out," Arlo snapped. "Get rid of him."

Felix stepped forward, his mouth wide in a shit-eating grin, reaching for the gun that Deacon now held.

"I'll do it," Deacon said, his tone like ice. He still didn't look at Rafe, but the words were enough for every hopeful cell in his body to wither and die. He tried to scramble free when Arlo let him go; he even managed to get a few feet away before Deacon's fist met his cheekbone and he crumpled at the strong blow.

"Don't kill him here like the last one," Arlo snapped. "Take him out like I fucking said."

"I'll take him to the lake," Deacon said, very clearly, concisely, as if he'd considered before now what to do with a body.

Deacon gripped Rafe's arm, yanked him into a standing position. The hold hurt – even more when Felix bound his hands behind him and Deacon dragged him outside. Down the stairs, through the back door, he was dragged and pulled, Felix at their side, every so often yanking at a part of Rafe as if he was helping. At the start of the dock, which vanished into the dark, he let his body sag, attempted to get away, but two men were holding him, two men digging their fingers into his arms and torso, and Felix's hand clamped tight over his mouth. He tried to bite, but it was getting difficult to breathe. Felix stuffed something in his mouth, and they must have reached the end of the dock, Felix letting go of him first and then Deacon shoving him backward.

"We should weigh him down," Deacon said. "I don't want him floating."

Rafe shook his head, looking behind him at the darkness beyond.

"I'll get something," Felix said gleefully, and vanished back the way they'd come.

Rafe spat out the material that Felix had stuffed into his mouth, but Deacon stopped him moving anymore, holding the gun at his temple just as Felix had.

Rafe coughed. "They killed my mom, after I was born – Arlo drove her car off the road." He was desperate. "And my dad – he knew what her brother had done, and for that they killed him too."

"Shut up," Deacon snapped.

"Deacon, you don't have to do this."

Nothing changed in Deacon's expression, and his gun hand didn't waver.

"I have to do this," Deacon said.

Rafe shook his head. "Please."

"I got these," Felix announced as he arrived back, and Rafe couldn't see, but he couldn't move either as rope was twined around his legs and the heaviness of something had him near stumbling. Felix stuffed the cloth back in Rafe's mouth, taking careful pleasure in pushing it deep.

Rafe tried to plead with Deacon with just his eyes. If only Deacon could help him, they could both get out of this.

"On the edge," Deacon ordered.

"Right on the fucking edge," Felix added gleefully.

Felix tied the rope around his hands, behind his back, pushed the fabric even further into his mouth, then looked him right in the eyes. "Bye, fucker."

And then he stepped away, and it was Deacon screwing on a silencer and aiming the gun at him, Deacon narrowing his eyes, aiming. His expression was dead – no emotion, no compassion.

And for the second time that night, Rafe closed his eyes.

* * * * *

The explosion of pain hit him so hard he knew he was dying, the force of it pushing him back into the water. The weights pulled him down, breath vanishing, his body nothing but a dead weight, and his last conscious thought was that at least he'd get to see his mom and dad again.

* * * * *

He was cold. That was all he could think. Death was cold. And it hurt like hell.

"Stay still, stop fighting."

The words sounded like his mom. Even though he'd never known her or heard her voice, he knew this was his mom, as an angel, in Heaven or Hell, looking after him.

"Jesus, we need to get him to a hospital." Another woman's voice.

Was it possible he was alive? The pain told him that he hadn't let go of life. If anything, the pain was screaming at him that he wanted to live.

"We have to hand this off," voice one said. She'd spoken a lot, close to him, talking at him, to him, about him, and all he wanted to say was that everything hurt.

"Ops won't like this."

"I don't give a shit; we don't know what he knows."

I don't know anything. I didn't find anything.

"I need you to clear the room."

This time a man was speaking.

"I'm not leaving," said voice one, the angel.

There was some banging, some cursing, and then the pain left him and he was in a blessed peace.

* * * * *

They made Rafe change his whole life – his name, his date of birth, his family history – and they made Craig Jenkins from the remnants.

Evie was his point of contact, a cop. She had taken a special interest in him, explained that they'd been monitoring the house and seen him go into the water. She'd rescued him, and he was grateful. So damn grateful.

He hated Evie by the end of his time with her, with the questions and the demands of what he should and shouldn't remember.

"Why do I need a new name? I want to go."

Evie showed him a video – a feed recording of Felix in a cell, his eyes wide, cursing and tearing at his hair, then stopping and looking right at the camera. "I'm coming for you, fairy. One day. One fucking day, you'll be mine."

Rafe watched the recording over and over; the man was insane, but when he said those words, he uttered them with absolute clarity and focus.

"I have notebooks," he admitted. "Stories my dad wrote down, about his suspicions that my mom was murdered years ago. Would it help to have them?"

Seemed to him that as soon as they sent someone to the bank deposit box, he could shed the last part of Rafe Ramirez.

That was when, with no other family and nowhere to go, he allowed Evie to mold him into someone new.

"What is your name?" Evie asked for what seemed like the hundredth time this hour alone.

"Craig Jenkins," Rafe answered, as he did every time.

"Date of birth?"

"September third."

"Where were you born?"

"Seattle."

"How old are you?"

"Twenty-three."

Over and over they made him say it, and for some parts of it Rafe actually opened his eyes.

CHAPTER 6

Three years later

"Beer?" Mac asked, and passed over a bottle before Deacon could say yes or no. Mac was good like that; he didn't ask questions when Deacon turned up at his door at the ass-crack of dawn, and he certainly didn't turn Deacon away.

He had encouraged his partner, Sam, to go back to bed; apparently Sam had only just come home from doing something to do with trees up on the mountain. He was bleary-eyed, but he managed a smile and a fist-bump before padding upstairs.

Mac opened a bottle for himself and led Deacon into the den, which had mostly sofas and a huge flat-screen TV. Mac didn't make Deacon talk; he simply sat on one of the sofas, put his feet up on the coffee table, and swallowed a healthy mouthful of beer.

Deacon didn't open his; he picked at the label and then, with a muttered curse, took a seat opposite Mac and hunched over his knees. The intel he'd received just after midnight had been enough to pour ice through his veins, and all those memories of three years ago had flooded him.

"I don't know where to start," he said, and picked up the beer, cracking the lid and taking a drink even though it was the last thing he needed right now.

"Are we killing someone?" Mac asked in a frighteningly calm voice. He did that kind of shit, with his utter focus and his sneaky Marine ways.

"No. Fuck, no." Deacon wanted to keep someone safe, not kill them. Not this time, anyway.

"Okay, so no killing, then, but I'm guessing you're not here looking for a bed and wanting bacon and pancakes for breakfast."

Mac's stomach grumbled at the thought; he was hungry, he didn't need beer, and he carefully placed the bottle on the table.

"It's all fucked-up," Deacon began. Because Mac would understand that; he knew fucked-up better than most men.

"How fucked-up? Are we talking as in personally fucked-up, or as in a huge conspiracy to take out the White House fucked-up?"

"You remember when I helped you with Sam and I said I'd just come off something intense?"

Mac nodded.

"I was undercover, a long time, finally managed to get into the Martinez family."

Mac whistled. "That was you?"

Deacon nodded. "My team, Evie and Lewis, and I were working the long game, had a tenuous link to the mayor's scandal from a few years before. Turned out Arlo was pulling the strings, had his hands in trafficking; drugs and human. He was a killer, and his son wasn't any better. They left a trail of bodies between them, but the son, Felix, he was mentally deranged, or that was what his lawyer had used to convince a jury. None of the murders could be pinned on him, always his dad, and he was put away for evaluation."

"Carry on."

"This kid shows up, right? Well, not a kid – he was in his early twenties, Arlo's nephew, had some plan to get inside his uncle's place and prove that Arlo killed his parents."

"I don't recall that part of it."

"You wouldn't. I killed him; took Rafe out of the equation before his name could be attached to the case."

Mac didn't blink an eye, didn't judge, only waited for more. That was what it was like to have known someone since they were in grade school; open and easy trust between them.

"At least I had to make it look like I had." Deacon patted his shoulder. "Aimed here."

"Your aim was always good."

"Long story short, my team placed him in witness protection, right? He's got some teaching gig about two hours from here."

"New identity, WitSec?"

"Yeah."

"So it's fucked-up how?"

"Felix Martinez, Arlo's son, and his twin Chumo, they got light sentences. Arlo took the fall for most of what had happened; died in prison third day of incarceration, heart attack after he learned that Chumo had died." Deacon pressed a hand to his side. "Chumo got a shiv, here. Someone didn't like his face I guess. Felix was locked up on psych ward, and he's gone."

"Gone."

Deacon still couldn't wrap his head around the lax security, the incompetence in the face of Felix Martinez, who was fucked in the head. His father had admitted guilt for everything, just to save his sons, but Deacon knew Felix had to have been responsible for so much more than anyone knew.

"And?"

Deacon reached into his pocket for his phone and scrolled to the image, passing it across to Mac, who looked at it carefully.

"White Hill Teacher, Craig Jenkins, Wins District Fight For LGBT Youth Club," he read out loud, and looked up at Deacon. "This is your teacher, on Facebook, the local media."

"Yeah."

"What the fuck was he thinking?"

"I don't know, but then I got a call. There's been an accident, a hit-and-run in his hometown, and he's in the hospital."

Mac's expression suddenly sharpened. "You think Felix saw the article, tracked down your teacher, this Craig Jenkins guy, and tried to kill him? How the hell would he have done that?"

Deacon didn't know what to say. "The cops are all over it. Even so, I don't like this." He hated to admit to Mac that he felt out of his depth, but Mac wasn't looking at him as if he was an idiot. He knew not to discount the feelings that Deacon sometimes had, that sixth sense that had got him out of sticky situations before.

"What do you need me to do? I can work the manhunt from my end. You take the teacher."

Deacon briefly closed his eyes. This was what he needed; someone to tell him he wasn't overreacting and that he had to be with Rafe, or Craig as he was called now. That was going to take some getting used to.

* * * * *

The hospital security was easy to get through with technical help from God knew who, passed on from Mac. Something to do with some agency called Sanctuary that Mac sometimes did work for. Deacon wasn't going to ask any questions or look a gift horse in the mouth.

He waited until dark to make his move to remove Rafe from the hospital. Within ten minutes of getting inside the entrance, he was up on the wards and had already assessed where Rafe – Craig – was being cared for.

He had to think of Rafe as Craig, had to recall the man was in WitSec and calling him Rafe would blow his cover.

Craig, his name is Craig. Not Rafe. Don't even think the word Rafe. Craig. Craig.

He'd discovered that *Craig* was pretty dosed up, with a broken leg and a missing spleen after internal bleeding. With a doctor's jacket and ID that he trusted no one would look too closely at, he was outside Rafe's door and steeling himself to push inside.

He could no more think of Rafe as Craig than he could kill him. He just had to be sure never to use his name. This could go one of two ways, just like most things in Deacon's life. Rafe could yell bloody murder, or he could maybe not recognize Deacon at all.

Deacon pushed a hand through his hair, longer and more styled than Rafe would recall, and certainly blonder – his natural color, not the dark blond-brown from when he'd been in character with the Martinez family. And he had less of a beard now; more like styled scruffiness, if that made sense to anyone but him.

His one regret from his time undercover was that Rafe's last look at him had been from the wrong end of a gun.

"He can be moved," a voice said in his ear. He had a comms device linked to Mac, who'd dug into medical records with help, and that was the message he needed to hear.

His plan was pretty simple. If Rafe needed to stay in the hospital, then Deacon wasn't leaving his side. If Rafe was okay to leave, then they were getting out now. Steeling himself, he opened the door, the wheelchair he was pushing banging the jamb. The room wasn't brightly lit, and Rafe seemed to be asleep, not stirring at the clattering of the wheelchair.

Deacon pushed the door shut behind him, and for a few moments he collected his thoughts and looked at the man lying in the bed. Gone was the softness of the twenty-three-year-old he'd known; this man was thinner, his features relaxed in sleep, his hands curled into fists on the covers over him. There were no cannulas, no machines, he was merely sleeping. Deacon moved closer, skirting the wheelchair, and leaning over Rafe. He pulled out the syringe in his pocket, a soft sedative, and injected it into the sleeping man's upper arm, the prick of it more than enough to make Rafe open his eyes, but they were unfocused as he blinked in the dim light.

"Wha'?" he said, flexing his arm and turning his head slowly to see what had woken him.

"Shhh," Deacon encouraged, and slipped a hand under Rafe's head, realizing his hair was way shorter. Gone were the layers and soft waves, and in their place his hair was short and prickly at the neck against his hands.

Rafe struggled, apparently aware of something being wrong, and then nothing – he was limp and pliable. Deacon maneuvered him into the chair and covered him with the blanket he'd stolen.

"You're clear," Mac instructed. "Take a left from the room, the service elevator, the car is in the loading bay. We can only give you ten minutes."

Mac sounded so reassuring, the tone of his voice enough to quell the fear in Deacon that at any moment someone could walk in and find out what he was doing.

He pushed open the door and looked outside. Nothing. Then, with feigned confidence, he followed the instructions he'd been given and kept a hand on Rafe's shoulder to stop him from slipping. There were cameras in the hall, but he had to trust Mac when he said they weren't recording him kidnapping a man from the hospital.

They made it to the loading bay without seeing a single person, and Deacon sent a small mental thank you to whoever Mac was working with who'd made this possible. Getting Rafe into the car was another thing altogether; he was so limp, and the cast got caught in the chair. In Deacon's head, ten minutes were ticking down.

A hand helped, and he looked left into Mac's face. Mac nodded grimly. "Three minutes – get out of here," he ordered, belting Rafe in. "Directions are in the GPS."

He remembered where Mac lived – that was the easy part – but he guessed it wouldn't hurt to have the soft voice telling him which way to turn if his worry for Rafe wiped out his ability to recall directions.

With only seconds of the ten minutes to spare, Deacon was on the road and away from the hospital, the engine of the SUV a soft, steady hum and his hands fixed firmly at ten and two on the leather steering wheel. Steepleshend, and Mac's place, was maybe two hours from here. He hoped the sedative would stay in place. Rafe breathed steadily, his head falling forward a little. Deacon pulled over when he was far enough out of town, and adjusted Rafe's seat to recline it, shoving his jacket between the window and Rafe's head as he slept the sleep of the drugged. As cars passed, their headlights shone into the SUV and highlighted Rafe's face.

He hadn't changed that much, apart from looking thinner. His lips were still the same, his ears, the faint marks of freckles over his nose. Deacon pushed his shirt aside. The bullet scar there, high on his chest, right into the fleshy muscle, as far from his heart as Deacon had been able to manage. He couldn't see the scar in detail, but it felt clean to touch.

When Rafe woke up he was going to kill Deacon.

And quite possibly Deacon would let him.

Sam was waiting as Deacon pulled up and went directly into Mac and Sam's garage. He came straight to the passenger side and cautiously opened the door, holding out a hand in case Rafe slipped.

"This is Rafe?" he asked, likely more for something to say than actually wanting to get confirmation.

"Craig – we need to call him Craig."

Deacon climbed down and went around, assisting Sam in getting Rafe out of the car, and between them they got him into a room near the back of the house. When they pushed open the door, there was a medical set-up in there, and a man sitting on a hard chair with his head tipped back and his arms crossed over his chest. He looked as if he was sleeping, but he moved quickly enough at the sound of them coming in, and between the three of them they got Rafe in the bed.

"Give me some room," the man ordered, and reached to touch Rafe.

Deacon covered his hand and stopped the movement. "And you are?" he asked, without holding back on the suspicion.

"Kayden, a friend of Mac's."

"Kayden's okay," Sam said. "Let's get a coffee."

Deacon released his hold and looked directly at Kayden, hoping to hell his expression was enough to ask him to look after Rafe.

Kayden gave a sharp nod, as if the message had been received, and Deacon was reassured that Kayden had this under control. He followed Sam out and into the kitchen.

"Who is he?"

"A medic for the organization Mac works for, Sanctuary. Kayden is a good guy."

Deacon subsided a little. If Mac trusted this Kayden, and he was a medic, then Deacon needed to be cool with it. They'd said he could take Rafe out of the hospital, but he looked deathly pale and his leg was in a cast. When he'd got a good look as they'd placed him in the bed, Rafe's entire body had been a mass of bruises and skin abrasions from where he'd scraped along the blacktop. He was seriously lucky not to have been killed.

Guilt suffused him, but he was there to keep Rafe safe, and not allow the guilt of what he'd done before distract him.

He'd been doing his job. Because of what had happened that night, he'd gained Arlo's trust, and that had quickly escalated. Within three months, he'd been able to bring the whole thing down – Arlo, his two sons, all locked away. Job done.

But he'd never forgotten what it had taken to get there. Couldn't lose the final image of a terrified Rafe falling into the water.

Kayden came into the kitchen, wiping his hands on a towel, his shirtsleeves rolled up and a look of grim determination on his face.

"Broken leg, bruising, his operation scar looks clean, his vitals are good. I've sedated him again, and it should kick in soon, but he's pretty drowsy. Thinks he's in the hospital, called me Doctor Meadows, very out of it."

"But he was okay to move – you said it was okay to move him." Deacon listened to himself, felt the panic in his chest. Maybe he should have left Rafe in the hospital.

All Kayden did was frown. "Of course he was okay to move." Evidently he didn't like that he'd been questioned. "I said so, didn't I?"

"Well, forgive me for not knowing who the fuck you are," Deacon snapped.

Kayden's frown dropped, and he shook his head. "Jesus, drama queen much?" he said, dropping the towel on the counter.

Deacon stepped into Kayden's space, wanting to ask and say a lot more.

In an economic movement, Kayden did this…thing, and that was the best explanation Deacon had, because he went from standing to lying flat on his back, winded, in an instant.

Then, to add insult to injury, Kayden toed his side. "He'll be fine. Stop thinking of him as if he's a baby; he's a grown man, healthy, he'll heal." Then he turned to Sam. "You know how to reach me."

"Thanks," Sam said.

Kayden looked down pointedly at Deacon, and Deacon looked back just as steadily, then gave a grudging thank you.

At which point, Kayden held out a hand to help Deacon stand. He took it, and for a brief moment had the idea of twisting and getting Kayden on his back on the floor, but the idea immediately fled. There was something dangerous in Kayden's soft smile, as if he was daring Deacon to make a move. Deacon was a former cop, and a freaking good one, but he didn't have the ninja going on that Kayden obviously did.

With Kayden gone, that left Sam and Deacon in the kitchen.

"What the hell is this Sanctuary? Are they all like that?"

Sam huffed a laugh. "No, Kayden's…special. He doesn't have time for anyone's shit. He's the brother of the owner of Sanctuary. They look out for people in need. I don't know much more than that, except that Mac does some work for them on and off."

Deacon nodded, then yawned widely.

"You should sleep," Sam chastised him. "You look like shit. There's a room on the second floor."

Deacon couldn't recall the last time he'd slept properly; probably right before the specter of the Martinez family had reappeared in his life.

"I'll stay with Rafe," he said. "Take the chair in there."

Sam sighed. "You know this is Mac's house as well. No one gets into town without being surveilled, let alone anywhere near the house."

"I'll watch Rafe."

"And if he wakes up and sees you sitting by his bed? You shot him in the shoulder and he still thinks you're a bad guy."

"I'll talk to him, reassure him. It will be fine."

Who was he kidding? Rafe would probably go into shock, and he thought maybe he could ask Sam to sit with him, but when he thought it through, he knew it had to be him. He wanted to be by Rafe's side. Whatever. And Rafe would listen when he woke up, and everything would be fine.

He turned on his heel, then remembered his manners at the last moment, turning back to see Sam watching him go. "Thank you," he said.

Sam nodded. "You're welcome."

Deacon settled into the chair next to the bed, watching Rafe sleep, searching his features in the soft light for any sign of the Rafe he'd known for such a short time.

The Rafe he'd kissed.

But knowing in his heart that the Rafe he'd known was dead.

CHAPTER 7

Rafe opened his eyes, attempting to focus on the ceiling above him. He tried to lift his hand, but it felt as if there was lead in his veins, everything heavy and he couldn't move. They'd told him he was getting better, so what the hell had happened? Had he relapsed? Why was he convinced that they'd taken him somewhere in an ambulance? That he'd leaned against a leather jacket that smelled of sunshine and soap? He blinked until the ceiling finally coalesced into the tiles he was familiar with.

Only there were no tiles.

Instead, the ceiling was a smooth white, and there were no strip lights, just a lampshade in a curious shade of blue. He blinked again. This didn't make sense.

But when he opened his eyes, nothing had changed. The ceiling was still white, the lampshade blue, and the drapes at the window matched the shade. The drapes. There were drapes at the window. Confusion morphed into panic and he turned his head to the right to get a better feel for where he was and he saw…him.

Sprawled awkwardly in the chair, his head back, long limbs this way and that, clearly too big for the chair, was a specter from a past that wouldn't leave him alone.

Deacon.

Intense fear sliced into Rafe.

They'd found him, had him strapped to a bed…was it Deacon who'd tracked him down and driven a car at him? He was paralyzed with a fear that made it hard to breathe, and he yanked at his hand, hoping to escape his restraints, only he wasn't tied down, there was no rope. Instead his hand came up fast and he rolled sideways. Catching himself and coming off the bed, forgetting the fact that his leg was in a cast and toppling sideways, falling with a crash into a cabinet. He flailed but couldn't stop himself falling, and he knew this was it – this time he was really going to die.

Deacon was up and at his side in an instant, and Rafe wanted to shut his eyes, wanted to block out seeing Deacon's face again as he died, but he had to watch. He wanted Deacon to see his fear, and maybe that would stop him; maybe he could make Deacon stop and think.

"Shit, Rafe— Craig," Deacon said, and reached for him, grasping his arms.

Terror became ice inside him, and Rafe stopped fighting; like a deer caught in headlights, he froze.

"What happened?" A second man stood in the doorway, someone Rafe didn't know – tall, dark and dangerous-looking. Maybe this new arrival could stop Deacon?

"Help me," Rafe forced out, looking past Deacon, scrambling to stand as the ice melted and he pushed himself to move.

"He woke up, saw me, and fell out of bed," Deacon said, and the other man came right in. There were two of them, and there was little Rafe could do to get away. There and then, he screwed his eyes shut; nothing was going to save him now.

But there was no pain, no bullet. Instead, the two men helped him to stand, and then he felt the bed at the back of his thighs and they sat him down.

"Are you okay?" Deacon asked. Even with his eyes shut, Rafe recognized his voice. He would never forget the tone of it, or the coldness of the man who'd tried to kill him. He said nothing.

"Open your eyes," the other man asked.

No.

"Craig? Rafe? My name is Mac. We're here to help you."

But fear was choking him and he couldn't breathe. "No," he managed between attempts to inhale enough oxygen not to pass out.

"He's panicking. What the hell did you do, D?"

"Tried to fucking kill him three years ago, remember?"

"Talk to him."

Rafe's chest was tight and he could feel the noose around his neck. He didn't want to die like last time. He didn't want to feel the bitterly cold water over his head, didn't want the panic, and abruptly he opened his eyes and looked right into Mac's.

"Help me."

"You're safe here," Deacon said evenly, his hands on Rafe's shoulders, pushing him down on the bed, holding him still.

Rafe pushed up against them, shoved him away.

"Help me!" he shouted loud, hoping someone would hear him.

"I'm not going to hurt you," Deacon snapped, and stepped back and away, his hands out in front of him in a gesture of innocence. "I'm saving you."

Rafe saw his chance. There was space between Deacon and the door, and he didn't even consider how far he'd get, but he wasn't giving up easily this time. He darted for the door, as much as a man in a cast could dart, and ended up running into the second guy, who rounded the door just as Rafe reached it. Desperation made him scrappy, but he wasn't going anywhere.

"Calm the fuck down," Mac said, holding his arms. Deacon was behind him, touching him. With nowhere to go and the inevitable ending only moments away, his body shut down and he let himself fall, scooting back as best he could and leaning against the wall. No point fighting. He'd spent three years looking over his shoulder, finally settled into a job, even begun to make friends. He'd been good at what he did, he'd been safe, and in the space of a few days, he was back here and about to die all over again.

"Give us a minute," Deacon murmured, and Rafe heard the door shut.

"Am I going to die?" Rafe asked softly, his words muffled in his hands.

"No, I promise."

"You shot me."

"I had to. I didn't want to." Deacon's voice moved away as he spoke, and Rafe opened his eyes to watch Deacon lean back against the bed. He sighed. "I was undercover, a cop, sent in to work the Martinez case—"

"You shot me," Rafe repeated. "You tried to kill me." He pressed a hand to his shoulder, recalling the pain, the fear, the water closing over his head. The word "undercover" meant nothing to him; he knew the meaning of the word, but where it applied to Deacon? He couldn't make sense of it.

"If I'd wanted to kill you…" he made a gun shape with his fingers and pointed it at his head, "I would have shot you right between the eyes." He immediately regretted his action when Rafe's eyed widened.

"I shot you in the shoulder so I could minimize the damage, but where the impact would send you back into the water, where my partner was waiting."

"Your partner?"

"Evie. She was the one who pulled you out. You remember that?"

He sounded uncertain, but Rafe absolutely remembered that. All of it. Every painful, terrifying, awful moment. He closed his eyes again.

"She was monitoring what was happening in the house. I said out loud that I was taking you to the lake. Can you remember me saying that?"

"Fuck you."

"I'm a cop," Deacon continued. "Was a cop," he amended. "I was undercover, and you were never supposed to be there. We were observing…shit, I wasn't even supposed to be in the house, and then you turned up, and they had to put me in so I could watch out for you. Only I ended up as your bodyguard."

Rafe gave a heavy sigh.

"You wanted to kill me," he repeated.

"They expected me to. You weren't the first person that had been removed; we knew your uncle was involved in three deaths of low-level drug dealers, we just couldn't prove it."

Rafe's chest tightened again. He wasn't going to trust a man who'd shot him. What he needed to do was get the hell away from Deacon and his crazy-ass friends. Evidence didn't point to Deacon killing him right at this moment, and Rafe didn't know what kind of game he was playing, but he'd go along with it until he could find a way out of there.

"Are you listening to me?" Deacon asked, his voice loud enough to pierce Rafe's thoughts.

Rafe nodded and scooted a little further away. "I'm tired," he said, and looked at Deacon steadily.

Deacon instantly looked contrite, stood, and extended a hand, which Rafe took before Deacon helped him to the bed.

"Are you hungry?" Deacon asked.

"No." Then Rafe pointed at the chair Deacon had been sitting in. "I don't want you staring at me."

"I get that," Deacon murmured. "I'll be outside."

"Where outside?" Rafe asked. "Listening at the door and watching me through a hole in the wall?"

Deacon alternated between bemused and affronted. "No."

Rafe shifted onto his side, however uncomfortable that may be, his back to Deacon. "Get out, then."

The door half-closed, and Rafe waited the longest time, dozing off between formulating plans to get away from Deacon. The clock in the room said it was three a.m. Outside the window, it was dark, and there wasn't much in the way of moonlight. He wouldn't put it past Deacon to be right outside the room, making sure Rafe didn't make a run for it. Not to mention the door wasn't entirely shut so he had to be extra quiet.

The only other way out was the window, and carefully Rafe curled up enough to swing his body weight up and off the bed without putting pressure on his bum leg. Every inch of him hurt, muscles twisted, skin bruised, not to mention the headache that banded his head. They'd reassured him he didn't have a concussion, but he didn't believe it for one second.

He yanked at a hoodie left in a pile of clothes on the dresser and attempted to pull on the sweats that went with it. At least they didn't have tight bottoms at the ankle, but still it was an exhausting task attempting to bend enough to be able to put them on. His surgery site ached like a bitch with the bending and pulling, and for a second he was winded and nauseated with pain.

The same pain he recalled when he'd been shot; a cramping agony that took his breath away.

There were no shoes, but he'd figure out what to do about that when he got out of the building.

After a few seconds of calming the hell down, he tested the window, convinced it would somehow be locked down, but it slid open easily. He examined the small drop. They were on the ground floor, and assessing his current ability, he sat on the windowsill and thought carefully about what to do next.

That was the kind of person he was. He thought long and hard about everything in his life, from deciding to go live with his uncle, to buying a freaking coffee. Consequences were always part of what he did, and the inevitable conclusion he reached at this point was that a non-graceful fall would be the only way out of there.

Something nudged his leg, and he let out a yelp before looking down to see a dog bumping him and softly whining. Where did a dog come from? Was he dreaming he was awake? He pushed it away and no, this was a real dog, then tried to get his leg up and over, but the pain banding his chest, his scar, his leg… He had no energy left to get out the damn window.

The dog bumped at him again and let out a low bark.

Shit. Damn thing will wake everyone up.

He reached down awkwardly and scratched the dog's head. "Hey, boy," he said, not entirely sure this was a male dog but knowing it was the friendly tone that was important. He'd had a dog as a kid; she'd be long gone over the rainbow bridge now. "Stay quiet now, right?"

"He's letting me know what you're doing." The familiar voice came at him from the room behind him, and Rafe's stomach sank. Mac.

He was stuck, halfway out of the window. No way would he be able to get out and outrun anyone with his leg in plaster, but maybe he could call for help.

"What do you want?"

"This is Cisco," Mac said, like he was just making conversation, and he stepped closer.

"I'm leaving," Rafe said quickly, leaning further out of the window. "You can't stop me."

"Okay," Mac offered pleasantly, and whistled low. Cisco left Rafe's side in an instant, coming to a halt right next to Mac, who was no more than six feet from Rafe.

"Okay?" Rafe was suspicious of that casually thrown-out word. Mac was probably biding his time, no doubt waiting for Deacon to come into the room and steal him back.

"Okay, you can go – no one is keeping you."

Rafe looked out at the dark, moved a little to center himself, but Cisco was there, gripping his pants leg with sharp teeth.

"Shoo," he said, and made a waving gesture with his hand. "Get your dog off me."

"He won't leave you unless I do." Mac's voice was way too close, and Rafe spun on his heel, which was hard and wrong and he nearly fell on his ass out the window.

"Tell him to stay with you."

"He'll stay with me," Mac confirmed, but then he stepped a little closer.

"You said I could go."

Mac nodded, as if he was agreeing that the weather was lovely, or that the food he'd just eaten was fine. "You can, but where you go, we go." He peered around Rafe at the ground outside the window. "You still in a lot of pain? I bet when the car hit you it was hard enough to throw you over the roof, eh? I know you lost your spleen, broke your leg, but I bet you're a mess of bruises. Not to mention sprains all over, and don't get me started on your intercostals. You must be in so much pain—"

"Jesus," Rafe snapped.

"Deacon's a good guy, you know," Mac said conversationally.

"Good at killing," Rafe snapped.

"He doesn't hurt the good guys," Mac pointed out.

"He killed me, for fuck's sake, so sue me if I don't think that's reassuring." Rafe's chest was tight and breathing difficult, and he realized he was losing control here. The night was cold and he was shivering.

Mac sighed and placed a hand on Rafe's arm and rubbed it gently. He tried to shrug free, but Mac wouldn't let go.

"He shot you to save you. He was undercover; he didn't want to hurt you. The people who want to hurt you, they're the ones he's protecting you from."

"No one is left who wants to hurt me," Rafe said. "My uncle and one cousin are dead, and my other cousin is on a psych ward. Who is left to want to hurt me?"

Mac sighed and finally let him go, then he stepped back and slipped off his jacket, handing it to Rafe. "Put this on," he said, "You'll freeze out there in just that hoodie."

Rafe took the jacket. "Fuck," he snapped, but slipped it on anyway. The decision was made; he was going out of this goddamn window, and he would find the first house he could and knock on the door, get inside to a phone and call the cops.

"I've got it from here, Mac." Deacon joined the weird group, the two big men and one dog in his bedroom.

"Hell, no," Rafe said, and leaned his body over, ready to fall out onto the ground, but Mac stepped forward. So did Deacon. It was Deacon who held him close and whispered in his ear the terrifying reason why this was all happening.

"Felix escaped and he wants you dead."

CHAPTER 8

Deacon felt the fight leave Rafe as soon as he said the words. He'd known they would have that effect.

"How? They told me he would never get out."

"He kept on his meds, found Jesus, fooled everyone, and ran."

"He killed people?" Rafe said, and shivered. "He hurt me."

"Let's get you out of the window and talk," Mac said.

"I'm tired," Rafe mumbled, and shrugged deeper into Mac's jacket. He didn't sound tired – he sounded as if he'd slipped into shock, and Mac made a hand gesture over his head and then melted away into the darkness, Cisco at his side.

Deacon put an arm around Rafe's shoulder, and he didn't flinch away, and that wasn't a good sign, because Deacon had seen the bruising all over his body from the accident. Deacon helped him back into the bedroom and shut the window one-handed. Rafe wobbled, and Deacon scooped him up as best as he could; the idiot was freezing. He carried him out of the bedroom and into the front room, deposited him on the sofa, and stepped back to look down at him. What could he say now? Should he explain about Felix, about the shitfest that meant the psychotic fucker was on the streets? Or the fact that Deacon had seen footage of the accident that had put Rafe in hospital, and there was a very high possibility that it had been Felix behind the wheel?

He went straight to the kitchen, made cocoa, grabbed blankets, and headed back to the sofa, where Rafe hadn't moved except to strip off Mac's jacket. Something about Rafe wearing that damn jacket had left Deacon feeling vaguely territorial. Go figure.

His eyes were still closed, and Deacon had a lot to tell him. He pushed blankets over Rafe, noticed his bare feet, wondering how far he'd thought he'd get outside without shoes, then moved a dining room chair to sit in front of him.

"Drink your chocolate," he said, carefully, quietly, waiting for Rafe to snap and hoping he didn't.

Rafe opened his eyes and reached for the drink, but his hand caught in the blankets and he stared down at it as though he didn't know what to do next.

Yep. Shock.

Deacon helped him again, and finally Rafe was sipping the hot, sweet drink and hadn't closed his eyes again. It didn't seem as he'd be receptive to talking, so Deacon waited a little longer.

Finally, the drink gone, Rafe looked up at him. Gone was the fear in Rafe's eyes, and instead there was the same steely focus he'd seen years ago back at his uncle's place.

"I drew a picture of you," Rafe announced. "I mean, not me really, but I gave your details to the police and they sat with me and we created this picture. I told them you shot me, that you tried to kill me, and they took me seriously."

"I know they did."

"But they didn't mean it, right? They were humoring me, keeping your cover intact."

What did Rafe want him to say? Did he want Deacon to deny everything at this point? What would make Rafe feel better?

"My cover was important."

Rafe huffed noisily. "I never saw daylight after they pulled me from the water; they had me in a hospital and Evie told me you'd gone. I guess she lied. Right?"

That wasn't so much a question as a statement of fact. Still, Deacon nodded. "Evie was my partner, my backup in this case, and she protected you from knowing it all."

"Protection? More like deception."

"Sides of the same coin," Deacon defended her, although Rafe's huff made him think that he wasn't agreeing with that statement

"How did Felix get out…when…why didn't Evie…or anyone tell me?" Rafe's words were a jumbled mess.

"I don't have the full details of what happened."

"Then tell me what you do know."

"All I know, all that Evie told me, is that he was in for an evaluation, he was determined, and he got out. He headed straight for you."

"How did he know…" Rafe looked confused, then the confusion cleared. "That article," he said. "I'm so fucking stupid."

"You should have been warned to keep your head down," Deacon reassured him. "Evie should have said."

"She did. I got the lecture, and the training, but this was important to me, and everyone who might have wanted to hurt me, they were all dead or locked away… Shit, I fucked everything up." Rafe sat quietly, then he stiffened, and that was the moment when Deacon could see it hit him what had happened.

"The accident?" he asked in a careful tone.

"I think it was Felix."

"He wants to kill me. Why? What's the point now?"

Deacon imagined that in Rafe's world, the bad guys stayed in prison, and the good guys got to live their happily ever after. Then it hit him how wrong he was. Rafe had seen his father killed, had never known his mother, and had deliberately thrown himself on his uncle's charity to find evidence to put his remaining family in jail.

"He is a murderer…"

"Okay," Rafe said, and pushed off the blankets holding him tight, standing up with the help of the sofa arm.

Deacon got up immediately, with a hand out to help him. "You need to take it easy."

Rafe ignored the hand and stood, albeit shakily, leaning to one side. "I'm going home."

"No."

"Call me a cab. I'm going home."

"What? No."

"Then give me a phone and I'll call a cab myself."

Deacon moved bodily to stop Rafe going anywhere, holding his upper arms, feeling the warmth of his skin under his touch. "Sleep now. We'll talk in the morning. Yeah?" He rubbed the warm skin, and Rafe's posture loosened a little.

"How did I even get wherever this is?"

"I brought you, as soon as I knew you were hurt and Felix was out there somewhere. I came and found you."

"Out of the hospital. What if you shouldn't have moved me? What if you'd killed me?" He looked right at Deacon. "Again," he added softly.

"You weren't in medical danger post-op and once they put a cast on your leg."

"I want to go home," Rafe said, his voice softer. "I already gave up everything once; I won't let it happen again. I have friends, I teach at a good school. I won't let my family take that from me again."

"You can't go home, Rafe – your identity is blown to hell."

All the fight seemed to leave Rafe, and he slumped.

"Get some sleep; we'll talk in the morning."

Rafe shrugged off his hold and used the sofa to aid him walking around Deacon, then with his back straight he limped to his room, the wall the only thing holding him up. The door closed behind him, and Deacon fought the instinct to go in and check if he was okay.

Deacon had shot Rafe, and lost the right to be that person who could follow him into a bedroom.

Mac cleared his throat from behind Deacon. "Was it the right thing to do telling him?"

Deacon sighed noisily and fussed Cisco. "Did you hear what he was saying?"

"He wants to go home. I get that; I would want to go home as well."

Deacon faced his old friend, the big, scarred man whose bravery had no limits, the one who'd seen and done so much. "He's not like you or me – he's a teacher, for god's sake."

Mac took a seat on the huge sofa and sprawled out, Cisco jumping up and curling next to him, and Deacon sat opposite. He had so many conflicting issues in his head, and he had to fix them, so maybe he needed to talk, and possibly the man he'd grown up with was the best choice.

Mac scratched Cisco's head. "One idea is you take him home and wait for this guy Felix to take another shot at him, and we take him out."

Horrified didn't cut it. "I'm not deliberately putting a civilian in harm's way."

Another door in the long corridor opened, and Sam came out, yawning. He stopped by the sofa. "What's wrong?" he asked, and didn't argue when Mac tugged at him and Sam ended up on his lap, Cisco shifting along as if this was a nightly ritual.

Something sharp poked Deacon's heart. He wanted that easy relationship, that simple, uncomplicated connection, and for a short time he'd wildly considered it with Rafe.

Rafe with his soft kisses and his plea that Deacon wasn't like the rest of them in that house.

Sam turned in Mac's arms and burrowed his head into Mac's neck, murmuring something and making strong, silent, angsty hard-man Mac laugh.

Seemed like tonight wasn't a talking kind of night.

"I'll leave you to it," Deacon said as he stood and stretched.

"We can still talk," Mac said, rubbing small circles into Sam's back.

"It's late, the security is up, but I'm thinking Rafe will stay in his room. Catch you on the flipside."

He bumped fists with Mac as he passed, and paused outside Rafe's door for a moment. He couldn't hear any movement, but he didn't need to worry about where Rafe was at any given time; the security in this house was at some crazy-extreme waiting-for-the-zombie-apocalypse level courtesy of Mac and his need to protect everything precious in his life.

In his room, Deacon undressed and lay back on his bed in his shorts. With his hands pillowing his head, he stared up at the ceiling. Tomorrow he had to make Rafe see that he was the one who would keep him safe; the one person who would risk everything to keep him alive. He didn't imagine for one minute it would be easy.

Nothing good in life ever was.

He must have slept, because when he opened his eyes again, there was faint dawn light coming through the windows. His first instinct was to check on Rafe, and he pulled on jeans and a T-shirt and padded down the stairs to Rafe's room. The door was ajar, and he looked in, pleased to see Rafe on the bed, curled into the covers, his face to the door, sound asleep. The painkillers were open on the bedside cabinet, and it seemed he had given in and taken some.

Deacon had coffee on pretty much immediately, Sam yawning widely and joining him a little after six.

"Couldn't sleep?" he asked, and took a mug of coffee with a grateful smile.

Deacon had a lot of answers for that one, reasons why it was important he didn't sleep, but in the end, all he did was nod. "You?" he asked.

"Dreams," Sam explained briefly. Deacon didn't push for more; Sam had seen some things in his time, traumatic incidents that he didn't talk about but that Mac had alluded to. "Mac is in the shower. How's Rafe – Craig – doing?"

"Sleeping."

Sam sat on one of the stools at the counter. "So what now?"

"We won't be here long," Deacon began, but Sam held up a hand to stop him.

"I didn't mean that – you can stay as long as you need to. I mean what now with the guy who wants to kill him? What do you and Mac have planned?"

"He has this insane idea about Rafe going back to his new life and waiting it out until Felix tries again." He still couldn't get his head around that suggestion. He was going to keep Rafe safe if it killed him, and keeping him safe meant hiding him away somewhere.

But Sam didn't immediately agree that it was an insane idea. He didn't jump in and point out that Mac was putting a civilian at risk and that there was no way Mac should even think that way.

Nope, he just sat there looking as if he was considering the concept.

"What the hell, Sam?" Deacon snapped. "You can't think it's a good idea to put Rafe out there as bait? He's a fucking teacher, for god's sake, not some undercover special forces guy with Mac's skills. Two minutes with Felix and a gun, and Rafe is dead."

Sam glanced past Deacon, but he didn't have to tell him that Rafe was standing there. Deacon just knew.

"Better dead than running away all the time," Rafe murmured, and brushed past Deacon, heading for the coffee. His gait was awkward with the cast and the crutch that Deacon had found him from somewhere, and the fact that he'd likely hurt himself the night before climbing out that damn window.

"I'll deal with Felix," Deacon said.

Rafe's shoulders sagged, and he turned to face Deacon. "Like you already did? Good job, by the way, on letting him get away with pleading insanity."

"You don't understand—"

"I don't?" Rafe cut him dead, looking stronger than he had the day before. His skin was pale, shadows under his eyes, and he was bent at the waist a little, like it hurt to stand upright, but he looked determined.

"Rafe, I just want to keep you safe."

Rafe hobbled over to him and poked him in the chest. Hard. "You don't get to decide what I do. Consider yourself off this case."

"This isn't a case," Deacon said helplessly.

"Then call it getting the fuck away from me and out of my life. As soon as I can, I'm going home, and you can't stop me." He poked at Deacon again, but Deacon grabbed his hand and held on.

"I'm not letting you go."

Rafe attempted to yank his hand from his grip, and only succeeded in losing his balance, stepping back to steady himself and catching his hip on the counter. He cursed and tugged again, and this time Deacon let him go, knowing the counter would hold him up.

"You," Rafe snarled, "don't *let* me do anything."

Rafe was fire and passion, and Deacon fought the instinctive need to pull him into his arms and hold on tight. He'd thought he'd never see Rafe again, had imagined that there would never be a point when they would need to meet.

But this?

This was touching, and feeling, and the lid that he'd put on his dangerous attraction to Rafe had slipped too far. He moved closer, saw the flash of fear on Rafe's face, the subtle tension in each line of him. Rafe was scared of him.

He backed away immediately, and ruthlessly pushed down any escalating affection he'd allowed himself to feel.

"I'll keep you safe from Felix," he said after a short pause during which Rafe stared at him with that same fear in his eyes.

Rafe's expression changed, then, from fear to disbelief. He shook his head in denial.

"It's not Felix who's worrying me. Who the fuck is going to keep me safe from you?"

He crutched his way out of the kitchen, mug in his other hand, coffee sloshing over the side and onto the floor. Deacon grabbed napkins and wiped it up, aware that sometime during that awkward exchange with Rafe, Sam had left the room.

Who could blame him?

Mac walked in, Cisco at his side, "Sam said—"

"Yeah," Deacon interrupted.

"What will you do?"

"Try to get him to see that he should stay here while I find Felix."

"He won't go for it," Mac said, helping himself to coffee and then filling Cisco's water bowl and weighing out kibble. Deacon watched his movements and waited until he was done before starting to talk again.

"He has to stay here. You didn't see what I saw at the end."

"Like what?"

"Three bodies in a back room, all shot point-blank." One of them Bryan, a kid with a stutter who tended bar. Arlo had killed them, or ordered it. Probably the latter, because Arlo never got his own hands dirty. From the violence done to Bryan, someone Felix liked to bully almost as much as he bullied Rafe, Deacon had always thought it was Felix who had been the blunt instrument that killed anyone in Arlo's way.

In his gut, Deacon knew it had been Felix; he'd seen the madness in the man, the willingness to hurt others.

"They were clearing up after themselves."

"Yeah."

Mac hoisted himself up onto the counter. "Your man won't stay here. He's got that look about him, as if he wants to face whatever he has to. I don't blame him, if this fucker tried to kill him."

Guilt pricked at Deacon. Rafe probably put him squarely in the camp of people who'd tried to kill him. Nah, there was no probably about it.

He sighed heavily and looked pointedly at Mac, wondering where this was going. "So what do I do?"

"Negotiate. Let us work on finding Felix first. Step back from the situation and understand what he wants and try to keep him safe while he's doing what he needs to do."

Deacon huffed. "Who died and made you clever?"

Deacon was the cautious one; Mac was a guy who lived on the edge, the one to start the trouble, and the one who never ran from the consequences. Mac lived and breathed trouble with a frightening control, which made him the perfect Marine.

"Sam insisted on climbing the damn mountain with me."

That wasn't a good comparison. "He was trained to climb mountains."

Mac frowned. "No, he wasn't, not as I was. But he was fucking brave, right by my side through everything."

"And you think the same thing about Rafe? It's not brave if it's stupid."

Mac hopped off the counter and stood really close to Deacon, tapping him on the forehead. "They're different sides of the same coin," he said as he tapped.

Irritability snagged at Deacon, and he caught Mac's hand, bending the finger back and shoving at him.

"Get out of my face, asshole."

Mac grinned at him. "Negotiate," he said one last time. "Now, if you're done with your angsting and shit, I have a wet, naked Sam to find."

He sauntered out of the kitchen, and Deacon couldn't even raise a sarcastic comment about not wanting to picture his best friend buck-naked in a shower. His brain capacity was too full of what the hell to do with Rafe.

Negotiate? He didn't want to be in a position of taking Rafe anywhere near a place where Felix could get to him.

So maybe Mac meant stall him. He'd said to give him a chance to find Felix, so all Deacon needed to do was stall him long enough to give them the time they needed.

How hard could that be?

CHAPTER 9

Rafe had known from the moment he'd been told his dad was dying over three years ago that his life was changed forever. He'd been called out of an ethics class, and at first he'd been pleased by the respite, not thinking that the Dean wanted to see him about anything other than his final year thesis.

"A terrible accident…a car…hit him as he crossed the road."

* * * * *

The cop who stood there telling him, a young woman not much older than himself, had huge brown eyes that were bright with sympathy. And the Dean laid a comforting hand on his shoulder when she'd left.

"You're a good student," Dean Rafferty murmured. "Your dad would be proud of you. I'll give you some time," he'd said, and left Rafe in the office with a view over the lawns of the college.

The Dean seemed to think that saying his dad would be proud was enough to balance the fact that his dad was now dead. Shame things didn't work that way. Rafe assumed the Dean had left him there to cry, but for the longest time – until three days after he got home from the funeral, to be exact – he didn't.

Until shock slipped away, and halfway through a lecture from his politics professor he felt something wet

on his cheek and realized it was tears. Stumbling out of
that lecture, with everyone staring, was the low point of
losing the protection of shock.

He went through every stage of grief; clinically, he
could even identify each one. Only after he'd worked his
way through all of them did he track back what had
happened. He knew his dad had gone to the West Coast,
knew he'd been going to talk to his wife's brother, Rafe's
Uncle Arlo, but how that had ended with him dying in a
car accident of some sort, Rafe couldn't figure at all.

Uncle Arlo had come to the funeral, with his quiet
wife and mean-looking sons, after they'd shipped Rafe's
dad back for cremation. He'd said all the right things, how
Héctor Ramirez had been the best of men, a good husband,
father and brother-in-law, working so hard to keep his son
on the right track. Rafe had believed him.

Then, a few days after, when Rafe realized he was
entirely alone, he acted on some of the things his dad had
told him, and he found the notebooks in a bank box. The
ones that either made his dad look like a madman writing
a crime thriller, or implicated him in knowledge of drug
deals that would destroy the memory of him forever. Rafe
wasn't ready to accept either reason, so he moved to
Arlo's home to find out the truth.

* * * * *

"Rafe?"

Deacon hadn't knocked, but the door was half open.

"What?" Rafe snapped. "If you've come to talk me
out of going home..."

"No," Deacon murmured, and stepped into the room. "I want to talk."

Rafe was suspicious of his tone, low and encouraging, and different to what he expected from Deacon.

"Yeah, right."

Deacon held up both hands. "If you want to go home, I can't stop you, but give it a week, heal some more, rest, and then I'll take you back."

"I want to go back now. I want Felix caught and I want him to pay for what he did."

"He'll pay," Deacon said, and there was a cast-iron conviction in his voice. "One week. Seven days. Records at the hospital reflect you signed yourself out AMA. Kayden will look in on you. No one knows you're here, and in seven days I will take you home."

Rafe's mind rebelled at the thought of agreeing to what Deacon was saying, but his body told him otherwise. He hurt. His stomach hurt, his leg ached, he was tired from lack of sleep, and he'd be safe here. Safer than he'd felt for the past few days.

"Three days," he said, and tilted his chin in a display of defiance.

"Six," Deacon said with a shrug.

"Three."

"Five, and that is where I stop," Deacon said, more focused, crossing his arms over his chest.

Could Rafe live with that? He called up the images in his head, of his father, and his mom, and the fact that he had neither here with him, and that Felix needed to pay.

But he was tired, and safe.

"Five days."

"Good."

"Saturday, I'm going home. I have a job, and school starts back on Monday. I want to be there."

Deacon gave nothing away in words, but his stance stiffened a little and he set his lips in a firm line. "Okay," he finally bit out. "Did you hurt yourself going out the window?"

"No," Rafe lied.

"That was fucking stupid."

"It was desperate," Rafe replied. *You tried to kill me. I don't trust you, but I have nothing else I can do right now.* "I want to talk to the cops."

"No." Deacon grabbed the back of a chair and turned it so he could straddle it.

"Get me a cop to talk to."

"No."

"One of the team that put me in witness protection. Evie – I want to talk to Evie."

"Rafe, listen to me. I need you to listen to me."

Was this going to be a fucking lecture? He didn't need lectures from some alpha asshole like Deacon. Still, he could pay lip-service and get the lecture out of the way so that Deacon would fuck right off.

"I'm listening."

"We don't know who helped Felix get out, or even if he needed help. We'll find out, but right now, your life is in danger and there will be no cops involved in this."

"Says the controlling asshole," Rafe muttered. "Surely the more people who know—"

Deacon stood up abruptly. "Five days. No cops. Get some sleep – you look like shit."

He left and pulled the door shut behind him. Fucker thought he was getting the last word. Rafe hobbled to the door and crutched out, past a startled Deacon, and through to the kitchen.

"I'm hungry," he said, and opened the nearest cupboard, which held, by luck more than judgment, cereal. Seemed like someone in the house liked their morning fiber – there wasn't a decent high-sugar multicolored cereal in there. He pulled out cornflakes and placed the box on the counter.

"You want some help?"

"No."

He found a bowl and pulled milk from the fridge. Awkwardly, with his crutch leaning next to him, he climbed one-handed onto one of the kitchen stools, holding back the yelp of pain at the pulling in his side.

And all the while Deacon watched him, irritation on his face.

"You're a stubborn idiot," Deacon said as he shook his head.

Whatever. Rafe had things to do, and he needed to eat if he hoped to heal enough to get back to his home, to his school. Slipping off the stool he took a bottle of water from the fridge, crutching past Deacon he had to give some kind of comeback.

"Takes one to know one," he answered, wincing at the stupidity he was displaying, and watched Deacon spin on his heel and leave the kitchen, muttering something under his breath about idiots.

"What am I?" he said to no one in particular. "Five?"

Back in his room, he noticed someone had been in and straightened his covers, the sheet taut on the mattress, the quilt pulled back at one corner. The drapes were drawn and the only light was the small bedside lamp. There were also meds right there on the table, and more water.

Sam? Mac? No, probably Deacon. Considerate bastard.

Rafe felt grungy, wanted a shower, however complicated that would be, but the bed looked so comfortable. So white. Swallowing some pain meds, he climbed onto it, his crutch toppling to the floor, and lay back on the pillows, staring up at the ceiling.

He'd move in a minute and get a wash or something.

When he woke, the room was in absolute darkness, no lamplight, and no sense that anyone else was in the room with him. He had no concept of the time, but he woke up needing a shower, or at least to splash water on his face. Cautiously, he opened the door, and from the darkness in the hallway he realized it must be night; he'd slept the day away. He opened the bathroom door and flicked on the light, blinking at the brightness, calculating carefully how the hell he was going to wash. Then he saw the note on top of a pile of plastic.

I know you'll want to shower. I know you won't ask for help. Wrap your leg in plastic, tape it. If you can't then please *ask Sam for help; he's in his office all day and he can come home. D.*

Rafe didn't need help. He could manage this. He didn't feel dizzy, and it had to be simple to tape up a leg in a cast. Surely.

After ten minutes, he finally stepped into the shower, tension in every line of him after the struggle to cover the cast and extra time covering the bandage on his operation wound, and a headache banding his head. The water was hot, and he relaxed under the steady stream, the heat of it clearing his head, and he allowed himself the luxury of thinking about nothing at all. No earth-shattering events, not the intense fear mixed with something else he couldn't identify that he felt for Deacon, not the fact that the dangerous-looking Mac was so openly affectionate with Sam, or that somewhere out there Felix was looking for him.

He attempted to forget it all.

Wrapped in a robe, he sat on the edge of his bed and peeled away the plastic protecting his stomach and his cast, checking if everything had stayed dry and thankful that it had. God knew what shit he'd have to listen to if he'd made the damn thing wet. Exhausted, he lay back on the bed, his feet still on the floor, closed his eyes, willing each of his muscles to relax, and he slept.

In his dreams, someone lifted his legs and turned him, and tucked him in. In his dreams, he told the person he was fine, that he needed sunlight, that it was daytime. In his dreams, someone sighed at him and touched his hair.

When he woke up warm in the darkness and tight under his covers, he knew one thing.

Deacon had been there, and none of it had been a dream.

Rafe realized he had no idea how to react to Deacon. Instinctively, he rebelled when Deacon got protective, and he couldn't bear to get too close to the man, because every time he got too close he remembered those last minutes on the jetty. He recalled Deacon's calm expression, the absolute certainty in his eyes as he aimed the gun at Rafe's chest and asked for something to weigh Rafe's corpse down in the water.

And the dreams weren't good, because they always ended in fear and sickness and screaming as water closed over his head. Intellectually, if he believed Deacon's story, then he needed to get over himself. Right? But what if there was doubt? What if his gut feeling told him that he couldn't trust Deacon? How was he going to get over that? And did he need to? Because after this was done, after Felix was caught, what would Deacon be to Rafe? A distant memory, that was all.

Evie arrived the third day he was there. She was all smiles and reassurance about how well he looked and how everything was fucking fine.

Only it wasn't, and he knew it.

"Why didn't you tell me about Deacon?" That was his only question.

She sighed and took the seat opposite him, nursing the coffee Deacon had made her before disappearing to give Evie and Rafe "time".

"What would I have said?"

"Something like, he wasn't a murderer, or a bad guy at all."

She looked at her coffee momentarily. "You have to have some bad in you to be effective undercover," she finally offered. "You have to be able to draw on something inside you to convince others."

Something bad inside Deacon? Maybe he should hold on to that thought. It would certainly help him come to terms with some of the hate and fear he had for the man.

"But Deacon?" Evie had more to say. "He thought so much of you, wanted to grab you and drag you out of that house and never let you go back. It broke him to see you in danger."

"Could have fooled me," Rafe muttered.

He listened as she extolled Deacon's virtues, and more than once the fact that he was a good guy. Seemed to Rafe that she thought if she said it enough it would sink in and he would immediately begin to accept who Deacon was.

"Tell me about Felix," he said, interrupting a story that no doubt would have included Deacon rescuing orphaned kittens in the snow or something equally heroic.

She blinked at him. "What do you want to know?"

"How did he get out? Why wasn't he in chains somewhere?"

"He killed a guard to get away."

And that was all Evie said, because she was the first to admit she didn't know how he'd got away so easily. Although a guard dying wasn't exactly easy. Another person dead because of Rafe's family.

He spent a lot of time in his room, when he wasn't walking circuits of the house on his leg, exercising the muscles, hoping to hell he could walk the pain away. It was on one of those walks, up in the attic, that he found the office space. Not a typical space, with a PC on a desk and maybe some pens and paper. Nope, this was high tech, and the door wasn't locked, so he limped into the space and sat on the first available chair. There were six monitors showing images of various angles on the house, the garden, the garage, the kitchen. Two other monitors with scrolling text that meant nothing to him, and which every so often was replaced by a representation of something on a radar, like the kind used by air traffic control. Then there were the computers. Three of them, all shiny and new, and none of them turned on at the moment. Whatever it was that Mac did, it was clearly some heavy stuff, and something that Rafe didn't want to get involved with.

"I see you found the Bat Cave," Deacon said from the doorway.

Rafe spun on his chair and knocked his leg on the table. He cursed in equal parts sudden pain and shock that he'd been discovered wandering into rooms he maybe shouldn't have. Deacon's expression changed immediately from one of teasing to one of serious worry, and he stepped closer before Rafe could stop him.

"Are you okay?"

"I'm fine; stop asking me that," Rafe ground out, even if the pain was shooting up his thigh and down from his scar.

Deacon came to a halt on the other side of the desk and forced his hands into his jeans pockets as if he didn't know what else to do with them.

"Are you?" he asked softly.

"Am I what?" Rafe was confused, which wasn't difficult at the moment with the pain and the drama and the rain of shit he was living under.

"Fine. You said you were fine, but you look as if you're in pain."

Rafe snapped. "Of course I'm in pain; a car drove right into me."

Deacon hunched his shoulders and guilt carved into his expression. "I know. I'm sorry."

"Why?" Rafe was abruptly pissed at this hangdog, guilt-ridden Deacon who was slap-bang in the middle of his life. "Why are you sorry? Did you let Felix out? Did you want to him to kill me? Do you know it was him? Or was it actually you? What is it that you're not telling me?"

Deacon stared at Rafe for the longest time, and Rafe could see the other man's brain working furiously. The Deacon he'd known at his uncle's place hadn't made thinking deeply quite so obvious. In fact, Rafe had pretty quickly judged Deacon as being a shallow muscle-man. How wrong he'd been.

"I didn't let Felix out – I don't know anything about that. I wanted him dead. I hated that he wasn't put away like his brother and father. But…"

"But what?"

"I had to shoot you."

Rafe didn't know what he'd been expecting, but it hadn't been that cold, blunt admission from Deacon. His chest tightened.

"You wanted me dead." That wasn't right. Deacon had explained that he'd been trying to make it look real.

Deacon grabbed a chair, turned it around, and straddled it. His expression was one of internal conflict, indecision.

"I wanted you out of there. You should never have been anywhere near that place, and I saw what they'd done to Bryan when we found his body, and I was fucking pleased I'd shot you and taken you out of the equation. They were going to kill you too, and if it had been up to Felix he would have beaten you to death. I had to control the situation, and I won't apologize for what I did."

"What happened to Bryan?" Rafe's voice was quiet. "I liked him. He was quiet and sweet."

Deacon grimaced, looking pissed that Rafe had even picked up on that particular part of the explanation.

"We found his body in the cellar after the raid. Along with others, all undocumented. There wasn't much left of Bryan's face; he'd been tortured. In his testimony, Chumo told the cops that it was his father's work, but I knew it had to have something to do with Felix. He was unhinged."

"Jesus."

"That could have been you, Rafe."

For a moment, Rafe considered the words, then he nodded slowly.

"But you didn't know that before you shot me, right?"

Why am I even arguing about this? I know Felix was out to hurt me.

"Rafe—"

"No, I know, I'm sorry. I think. I don't know who the fuck I'm even apologizing to. Is it the cop? Or the man I knew who dealt with my uncle's problems? Maybe it's the man who kissed me or the one who shot me. I have no fucking clue anymore."

Exhaustion stole over Rafe, and he scrubbed at his face with his hands; his head hurt and he couldn't make sense of any of this.

"I'm not running," he mumbled into his hands. "If it was Felix who pointed a car at me, then I'll face him man-to-man, and we'll clear up this, and the cops can arrest him."

"And I'll be right next to you."

That made Rafe look up. "What if I don't want you there?"

Deacon shrugged and crossed his arms over his chest. "What if you have no choice?"

For a moment, Deacon waited, as if he was expecting an answer from Rafe, then he moved to the side wall and unclipped a bracket that unfolded out to reveal what Rafe could only think looked like one of those boards you saw in cop shows. Pictures and lines drawn in different colors, and right in the center of it was an image of him. Grainy and evidently taken from a distance, it sat in the middle of grid and had various lines leading from it.

He pushed himself up from the desk, grabbing his crutch and awkwardly stumbling around the desk that had sat nicely between him and Deacon, protecting him. He came to a stop in front of the board. There was so much detail. Lines to his parents, with remarks next to each picture, cold clinical facts, date of death, cause of death. He inhaled sharply at the pictures and glanced at Deacon, who stared at him.

"I didn't know when to show this to you," he murmured.

Then he tapped at another line from Rafe's picture, tracing it to a part of the board with his uncle's name and those of both Felix and Chumo, the twin's pictures near identical. When you knew them, you could see small differences, like Chumo was softer, Felix manic, Chumo smiled more, Felix was bitter. But in the end, the twins had an equal amount of evil in them, Felix's had just been closer to the surface. Chumo was sly at times, allowing his brother to take the brunt of anything physical and collecting up any leftover crumbs of praise from their dad.

Deacon tapped the picture of Arlo again. "Arlo Martinez. When he arrived in the US, he had nothing."

"I've heard this story before," Rafe said. "Moved to LA, worked construction, made money that way."

"That's half the story. Construction was a cover story for most of what he did, the gray areas, and in 2012 there were several arrests for embezzlement of city funds in the town he'd settled in – the mayor, his staff, giving themselves huge salaries at the expense of the town. But they never linked it to Arlo, even though it was he'd bankrolled some of the nastier things they were into. They wanted someone inside, and that was me; I was undercover for two years, working my way sideways. The end game was always taking down Arlo, working out his supply routes."

"Supply routes for drugs?"

"Yeah, and worse. Human trafficking."

Rafe's legs were like rubber; they wouldn't hold him up. "What?"

"We need to find Felix. Is there anything you can add to this board that might lead us to where he is?

"Nothing."

He was lying. Well, half lying. He had no idea where Felix could be, but he did have things that could fill in gaps. But what was the point in sharing anything like that now? His dad's secrets deserved to be left where they were.

"I don't know where he is." He pulled back his shoulders. "But he found out where I was, and I need to go back there. To finish this."

Deacon nodded mutely. He didn't look happy at the thought. Then he walked out of the room and left Rafe standing there, staring at the information wall.

Alone, Rafe pressed his fingers to his lips and then to the picture of his parents together.

Today, right here and now, he missed his dad and wished he'd known his mother.

CHAPTER 10

Deacon had to walk away. To hear Rafe say he had to finish things, to think it was a good idea to go home, where he could be seen and maybe hurt, didn't sit well with Deacon at all.

For a while he paced the hall at the bottom of the stairs, wishing Mac or Sam were there. But Sam was at work and Mac was off attempting to find Felix. So far, Felix was proving elusive, and Mac hadn't found hide nor hair of the asshole. Still, at least with Mac out there working that angle, Deacon was here, able to look out for Rafe.

He paced some more. Looking out for Rafe was a fucking joke. The man wouldn't listen to him, so how was he supposed to keep him safe? Why wouldn't Rafe simply agree that Deacon was the cop here – ex-cop – and that he knew what he was doing?

And why had Rafe sat in that room and looked so damn guilty, as if he knew something he wasn't telling?

By the time Rafe came down the stairs, Deacon had worked himself up to a full head of steam, temper sparking inside him.

"What's the fucking point?" Deacon shouted at a startled Rafe, who stumbled on the last step and had to grip the wall so as not to end up on his ass. Somehow that made everything worse, because, fuck, now Deacon could add even more guilt to the growing pile he carried around with him.

"What?" Rafe asked when he had his balance.

"I should have just let Felix kill you back at the lake, then I wouldn't be here trying to save your ass all over again. Do you realize how many people could have died if I hadn't shot you, if for one minute your uncle had thought I was anything else but a gun for hire?"

"Deacon—"

"The next night, my team rescued twenty-three illegals, crammed in a van – women, kids – and it was after I passed on my intel." He stepped closer to Rafe, and could see that his words were hitting home. "My intel, because I stayed in character. And that wasn't the last of it. Within a month I had them all arrested, a total of fifty-six souls saved, not to mention cutting the drug supply that your uncle had going to local distributors and then on into fucking schools. Kids. Right? I saved them, but to do that I had to take you out of the picture without breaking character, and I didn't want to – I wanted to yank you out of there, break my cover, and save you alone. Never mind the others. You made me do that."

He knew he was being irrational. But hell, irrational felt good right about now.

"I didn't make you do anything—" Rafe began, but stopped when Deacon stepped right up into his space, hardly any room between them, so close Deacon could smell the shower gel Rafe had used that morning and see the ring of darker color in the green of his eyes.

"Yes, you did. You should have listened to me, turned around and left—"

Rafe stiffened. "He killed my dad—"

"And he could have killed you!" Deacon shouted, and Rafe winced. Guilt and anger and need all collided in one perfect moment, and Deacon snapped.

He hauled Rafe close, angled his head, and kissed him. Hard. With no finesse. It was all lips and heat and hard teeth and tongue, and it was the best taste of passion and fire he'd ever had, and at first, for a moment, Rafe was immobile, letting the kiss happen to him.

Then it changed, and Rafe met Deacon for every kiss, the crutch crashing to the floor and Rafe linking his arms around Deacon's neck, letting Deacon take the weight of him, and god, the weight of Rafe was perfect. Deacon stumbled back, taking Rafe with him and finding a wall, any goddamn wall, twisting so it was Rafe pinned there, careful of his operation site, and his hurt leg, and he was so hard. The kisses grew more desperate, not gentling one little bit. This wasn't romance – this was life-affirming fire and temper, and Rafe groaned into the kisses, his hands leaving Deacon's neck and sliding into a new position, grasping Deacon's ass and grinding against him.

I should stop. What am I doing?

Deacon attempted to pull back, to give Rafe time to think, but Rafe cursed at him, his eyes closed and his grip hard. And Deacon could no more stop than he could cease breathing.

He'd known Rafe would taste like this; he'd fantasized about having the man beneath him again. Fucking him, swallowing him whole…it was as if Rafe was under his skin and no amount of scratching the itch would ever get him out.

Deacon pushed hard to back away a little, getting his hands on Rafe's loose sweats and onto his hard cock, wrapping his fingers around it and kissing Rafe as if there was no tomorrow. Rafe broke the kiss, whimpered, and Deacon looked at his face, the concentration there, the absolute focus as he used Deacon's hands to get off. When he came, Deacon was moments after him, just at the expression on Rafe's face, the utter bliss, mouth open, eyes still screwed tight shut.

When was the last time he'd come from kissing alone? Ever? He couldn't remember.

They leaned on each other, both breathing heavily, and some part of Deacon never wanted to let Rafe go.

Only that wasn't going to happen.

Rafe shoved him, his eyes open, and there was something in them – regret, shame, fear? Hell if Deacon understood what he was looking at.

"Rafe?"

Rafe stumbled around him, and Deacon helped by picking up the fallen crutch and passing it to him. Then, when he thought Rafe might start a conversation, he simply turned and left.

"We should talk," Deacon said quietly, and Rafe stopped at the top of the stairs.

"No," he murmured, then left Deacon standing there, his pants wet with come and his head full of regrets. The first time should have been soft lights and music and wine and all that fancy shit that defined romance. It shouldn't have been rough and hard up against a fucking wall when anyone could have walked past them.

Deacon's stomach fell, and he leaned back on the wall he'd just got off against.

He was a mess; no wonder Rafe had walked away from him.

Things weren't any better when he went downstairs and found no sign of Rafe apart from a shut door to his room. For a second he imagined Rafe had gone, but security hadn't been alerted to anything, so Deacon had to assume that Rafe was safely in there with his regrets and the shame of what they'd just done.

Sam came through the front door, shrugging off his jacket and toeing off his boots, then padding into the kitchen, where Deacon had been watching him.

"Hey," he said, and went straight to the coffee machine. For a while he said nothing, then he turned to face Deacon. "What is it?" he asked a little fearfully. "Why aren't you saying anything? You look odd. Is it Mac? Is he hurt?"

Deacon wasn't following anything there, and then he put two and two together. He was lost in his own headspace and probably had an expression like death. "No, Mac is fine."

Sam wasn't backing down. "Then what's wrong?" he asked suspiciously. "You look like shit."

"Thanks for that," Deacon deadpanned, then looked down at himself, hoping to hell there wasn't some wet patch right there for Sam to see. Thankfully, his shirt was untucked and covering anything that needed to be hidden away. Then he looked up, and Sam's eyes were narrowed.

"What. The. Hell. Happened?" Sam asked insistently.

Deacon knew he could handle this one of two ways. The first option was to lie, the second was to lay the whole sorry mess he'd just made on someone who was sleeping with his best friend. Neither option sat well with him.

"Rafe and I had a thing," he explained, and hoped that was enough.

Sam sighed and turned back to the coffee. "You two are like a walking mess of UST."

"What?"

"Unresolved sexual tension," Sam explained.

"I know what UST is, but what do you *mean*?"

"He stares at you when you're not looking as if he wants to know what's going on inside you, as if he wants to devour you whole."

Jeez, talk about fanciful. "That's probably the drugs and the pain," Deacon said, and took a mug from the cupboard, waiting patiently for his turn at the machine.

"Whatever. It doesn't help that you look at him the same way. Just how far did you take things when you were undercover?"

Deacon didn't know if that was any business of Sam's – what happened on an undercover assignment stayed there – but this wasn't his home, it was Sam's, and Sam was Mac's partner, and by extension Deacon should be able to trust him.

"I tried to stay away," he said softly, and took his coffee to the table, sitting as usual facing the door.

Sam stayed where he was, leaning against the counter, nursing his coffee, and not for the first time Deacon noticed that Sam looked tired. Two nights in a row he'd found Sam in the main living room, sitting on the sofa, watching infomercials. He missed Mac, worried about him when he wasn't there, couldn't sleep.

"But you couldn't – stay away, I mean."

"He went into that place thinking both his mom and dad had been killed by his uncle. He willingly put himself inside that part of his family to try to find evidence to prove what his uncle had done. He was so brave, but I didn't want him there."

"Don't start with the civilian thing. I hear that from Mac and it pisses me off."

"What?"

"You're going to start some crap about how Rafe is a civilian and should leave all the heroics to the big bad 'special forces' guy." Sam air quoted the words with his free hand.

"Not special forces, I'm a cop," Deacon began. "Was a cop," he corrected. That title wasn't his anymore, not for two months now.

"Cops, marines, SEALs…you're all the same, all with huge hero complexes. Which, yeah, it's a good thing because it keeps people safe. I get that. But it also means you have this thing about everyone else needing to be looked after. Rafe can be brave and a hero in his own right. He didn't put himself in harm's way to get killed; he did it to find closure for his dad."

Deacon stared at Sam, thinking on his feet for some argument that would prove Rafe should stay in his room, all safe, preferably wrapped in blankets and heavily sedated until this was all over. He had nothing. So he sighed, then smiled wryly.

"I bet Mac hates it when you use logic on him."

Sam grinned widely and saluted Deacon with his mug. "Every damn time."

Deacon's stomach rumbled, reminding him he'd skipped breakfast and was well on the way to passing lunch, and he opened and shut cupboard doors and the fridge, finally piling up the makings of bacon sandwiches, nectar of the gods. Sam excused himself, said he'd eaten, so it was just Deacon and Rafe. Armed with coffee and sandwiches, he hovered outside Rafe's door, then tapped it with his foot.

"Lunch?" he called through.

"Go away," Rafe said, very clearly and firmly.

Fuck that shit. Using his elbow, he pushed the handle and eased his way in, sloshing coffee on his hand and holding back the curse. He expected to see Rafe under his quilt in darkness, but the room was filled with light, the drapes pulled, clothes neatly piled on the bed, and Rafe in nothing but a towel, with wet hair.

"You showered," Deacon observed, just for something to say.

Rafe nodded. "I felt dirty," he murmured.

The weight of the admission pushed Deacon into the ground, but he didn't let it show. Carefully, he placed the sandwiches and coffee on a side cabinet and left the room, closing the door behind him, feeling nauseated. Guilt ate at him. He was the one who'd forced himself on Rafe, not given him the chance to say no. He'd clearly misread all the signals he thought he'd felt and seen. Maybe Rafe hadn't been holding tight. Maybe it had been something completely different.

He walked straight past the kitchen, ignoring his lunch and stalking out into the garden to get some fresh air.

Him.

He'd been the one to start all that shit against the wall.

And he was the one who'd made Rafe feel dirty.

CHAPTER 11

Rafe ate the sandwich and drank the coffee, got dressed and sat on his bed. He had the feeling that he'd somehow fucked up. Seen the light go out of Deacon's eyes, replaced by hurt and guilt as he'd spoken.

"I felt dirty," he said to his room. "Who even says shit like that?"

He just knew that if he hadn't said something, he would have dropped his towel and climbed all over Deacon, because, shit, he'd never come so hard or so fast in his life. His entire life. Not even the first time at fifteen, which had been more awkward fumbling than mind-blowing sex.

The expression on Deacon's face; he'd looked shocked, guilty, and then he'd left. Just walked out.

"Dirty," Rafe muttered, and buried his face in his hands. Suddenly, climbing out of the window and limping away from there seemed like a perfectly valid reaction to what had just happened. He owed Deacon something right now – an apology, or an explanation, or *something*. Deacon seemed to carry around the weight of the world on his shoulders, and now the shock was subsiding over seeing the man again, maybe Rafe could get some perspective.

"I can go out there and tell him that I'm okay with him shooting me, and that I'd like to kiss him again. And that I want to go home now."

If he expected the room to answer back, then it wasn't happening.

He closed his eyes and wanted to focus on being pushed against the wall and made to feel, but all he could see was the blackness of the water as it closed over his head. All he could imagine was the pain and the certainty that he was dead. Life was supposed to flash before your eyes; he didn't recall anything like that, just the blind terror of dying.

Would he ever forget that, split it away from Deacon?

Had he begun to do that already?

Determined, he crossed to his door and threw it open. Deacon was standing on the other side of it, his fist raised to knock.

"I'm sorry."

"I'm sorry."

They spoke at once, but Rafe had to get in first. Had to explain.

"I didn't mean you made me feel dirty. I just meant that I wanted a shower, that I felt grungy— Shit, no, not because of you or what we did. Fuck, that was hot, and I want to do it again, but I want to go home, and I want to be better, and I want this to be over."

He stopped and waited for Deacon to say something, anything at all, and watched the expressions play on his face. He went from contrite, or at least that was what Rafe thought it was, to a frown, then right to a smile.

"I'll get you home," he said. "Saturday, as we agreed."

Rafe knew he was playing for time in the hope that Mac would find Felix, but why would Felix even stay around Rafe's new home? Surely he would have chalked

Rafe up as a loss and made a run for it. Preferably to another continent.

"Okay."

"I am sorry, though," Deacon continued, "about what happened just now."

Rafe's chest tightened and shame began to build inside him. Here was Deacon, standing there apologizing for something that Rafe had thought so absolutely perfect.

"It's okay," he said, just for something to say and to let Deacon off the hook.

Deacon stepped into the room, Rafe moving back a little, then Deacon closed the door behind him.

"Come here," he begged.

Rafe was pulled closer by some invisible cord, the shame leaving him and the tension between him and Deacon crisp and clear. When they were so close they were touching, Deacon cradled Rafe's face and guided him to look up at him.

The kiss was gentle this time, a press of lips and then deeper. This wasn't a kiss to go along with frantic rutting against a wall, this was a kiss that meant something real. A connection or a promise. They kissed forever, and it still wasn't long enough, Rafe carding his hands through Deacon's thick hair then holding tight. Deacon's hands moved, rested on Rafe's hips, holding him still, the two of them hard against each other.

And then he gently eased Rafe away and the forever-kissing stopped.

Rafe was bereft and chased for more kisses, but Deacon stopped him with a smile and a subtle shake of his head. For a second, Rafe considered listening to him, but then he thought one thing. Fuck it.

And he was back, pressed against Deacon, and he ignored the pain in his side and the ache of his leg; all he could do was focus on this one point.

He heard Deacon groan into the kiss, and he might not feel like fucking against another wall, but he was lost in the sensations of how goddamn nice this was.

CHAPTER 12

The vibration of his phone woke Deacon, and he eased away from Rafe, who didn't stir a single inch.

Padding out of the bedroom, he answered the call after seeing Mac's name on the screen.

"This is big," Mac said without introduction. "There are numerous agencies after this guy now. Sightings in Saco and Portland. At one point they closed in on him, but he'd gone. There's more bodies, D. A hooker and a cab driver."

Deacon closed his eyes. "They think—"

"There's no thinking. He's blatant about what he's doing and he's been caught in various surveillance shots. I'm sending everything to your phone."

"What about the place you work for? What is Sanctuary doing on this?"

"Chasing as many leads as they have. Between us, we'll get him, D. Get some sleep."

Mac ended the call, and Deacon waited for the information to arrive. What he saw made him feel ill. Felix was sick. The hooker looked like she was asleep, apart from the line of scarlet across her throat. On the other hand, the cab driver was unrecognizable, as if Felix had gone to town on him. In fact, the cab driver, sprawled on the sidewalk, looked like Bryan back at the Martinez House; beaten to death.

He read the reports and flicked through photos. Felix wasn't hiding his face. City cops were on his back, the feds, a team from the unit he'd been incarcerated in, and Mac with his Sanctuary backing.

But it wasn't enough, Deacon knew that.

Somehow, Felix was slipping through the gaps, sidestepping anyone who could stop him, and he probably wanted to finish Rafe.

Deacon closed his phone, then his eyes, and for a few moments he sat in absolute silence. Then he pulled his gun from the holster and checked the bullets inside it. Checking the windows and doors one more time, he berated himself for not thinking this through. Felix was in the city, but that was no more than a couple of hours from here.

He scouted the blueprints of Rafe's place in preparation for their arrival. How secure was the bakery below this apartment? What about fire? Was there a way out of this place if the stairs were blocked? He scouted the various escape routes, found a couple of options he was happy with, and then there was nothing else he could do.

He crept back into the room, Rafe still sleeping, and curled back into the position of big spoon, holding Rafe protectively close to him. Felix would have to go through Deacon to get to Rafe.

Deacon didn't sleep again, and Mac arrived at the door a little after four a.m. He looked resigned, focused, and gestured for Deacon to shut Rafe's door.

"We need to talk about you and me finding this man and putting him down ourselves," Mac began without introduction. "If we could get him to come here?"

"Why would he come here again? He has to know there will be people waiting for him." Deacon saw the quick change in Mac's expression and was filled with horror. "No," he said, "We're not using Rafe as bait." He didn't want to hear that putting Rafe in harm's way was a good idea, or that the only way to stop a madman was to put the man he loved in the path of danger.

The L-word. He slumped onto the sofa, dejected, overwhelmed, and wondering when in hell his life had taken this turn.

The minute Rafe looked at you the first time he met you. That was when everything changed.

"It might be the only way, D," Mac murmured. "People are dying."

"I can't, I love him," Deacon said softly. Then he looked at Mac. "I love Rafe."

"I know." Mac sighed and took the seat opposite. "And that is what makes everything so much harder." He paused and wriggled a little, a familiar gesture that Deacon remembered from when they were kids.

Mac was tightly wrapped up, impenetrable, and when he felt as there was any chance he'd show weakness, he wasn't able to just be still. He wriggled and looked like he'd rather be a million miles away.

"The minute I admitted the way I felt about Sam, I was done. I've seen so much hate in this world that I wanted him to stay at home, all the time, every day, not work, just stay here, safe. He got into here," Mac tapped his chest, right over his heart, "and the thought of seeing him hurt or in danger…"

Mac didn't need to continue; Deacon understood being exposed. He'd spent so much time cultivating the hard undercover cop that he'd never stopped to think about letting anyone in. Loving someone made you vulnerable, so he'd never fallen in love.

"Then I met Rafe," he said out loud, but he didn't need to explain the rest, because Mac was nodding and looking thoughtful.

"Remember the treehouse in your yard back in Mass?" he asked.

Deacon blinked at his friend, not following the change in conversation. Medford, Massachusetts, the treehouse in his sprawling backyard. He hadn't thought about that in a long time. The last thing his dad had built before cancer had stolen him away. He and Mac had spent hours up there, playing cops and robbers.

"I remember," Deacon said.

Mac laughed. "I tried my first judo moves on you—"

"You never brought over enough snacks—"

"You never wanted to be the bad guy—"

"You used to eat everything I took up there." Deacon huffed.

"You made me eat a worm." Mac looked horrified at the memory and gagged a little.

"You said you could survive on nature," Deacon said, and shrugged.

"Not worms."

They grinned stupidly at each other, everything happening around them forgotten.

"Being ten was all kinds of awesome," Deacon said.

"Except for the fights we had, about who would play the bad guy, because even at ten we had these ridiculous hero complexes." Mac shook his head. "Sam called me on it, said I needed to stop treating him like the one who always needed saving, because you know what?"

"What?"

"Sam is perfectly capable of saving me right back."

Deacon opened his mouth to tease Mac, but saw the honesty in his best friend's eyes. Was that what Rafe was doing with him? Saving the rough cop one kiss at a time?

"That doesn't mean you would let him be a target."

Mac continued, "Rafe is strong, and with us backing him up, we can smoke this Felix guy out and keep him safe all at the same time."

"Would you put Sam in this situation?"

Mac paused, then leaned forward. "I wouldn't want to. I would fight it every step of the way, but yeah, I would have to, because the alternative – not facing this head on – would leave the man I love in danger. Not to mention all the others this psycho will kill."

Deacon wanted to call bullshit, but he knew Mac, and this wasn't bullshit at all.

"What kind of backup can we get?" he finally asked.

Mac nodded; clearly he approved of moving on to the strategy side of this heart-to-heart.

"Not much, but we'll have what we can work with."

"I don't want Rafe in harm's way. How many people has Felix killed now?"

"What?" Rafe's voice told Deacon that he was wide awake and standing behind them. Deacon sank in his seat; he'd assumed that Rafe would be asleep for a while. "What's going on?"

"Nothing—"

Mac interrupted whatever Deacon had been going to say to get Rafe to go back to bed.

"Felix is in Portland, and authorities believe he is responsible for the murders of at least two people."

Deacon died a little inside. Why did Rafe have to know? Why did he have to face the choice of making himself a victim just to take this fucker off the streets?

"I want it done," Rafe said, and joined them on the sofa. "I want to face off against Felix, and then it's finished. He comes after me, you're waiting, it's done."

Rafe's voice was flat, but his expression was determined.

"No," Deacon said. "I won't let you do that."

Rafe looked right at him. "You don't have a choice. Mac, get it done. How do we get him here?"

"An interview, maybe? Anything to get your visibility up so he knows you're here."

Deacon could do nothing except listen as Mac and Rafe went over the options of things they could do to get Felix there.

Then Mac left, and abruptly it was just him and Rafe, and he didn't know what to say.

"Why would you agree to this?" he finally said into the silence.

"Because I don't want more people to die because I'm scared. We know that someone else could die because of me, and I won't let that happen."

"Never because of you. Felix isn't killing because of *you*. He's killing because he's a murderer."

"I want to do this. I'm going to do this, whatever I can to get him to come to me, so you and Mac can take him down."

"Jesus, Rafe. Give me a minute to just think," Deacon snapped.

"Think about what?" Rafe shouted back at him. "How many people should I let die before I go home?"

What? No, that wasn't what he was doing. "Jesus, Rafe, no."

"Well, are you weighing up the pros and cons of other's deaths compared to mine?"

"No. Stop it, let me think." Deacon shook him a little, and Rafe yelped at the sudden tug in his side, meaning that Deacon let go of him. "Shit, I didn't mean to hurt you."

Rafe looked as though he didn't know what to say. He pressed a hand to his side, and Deacon was flooded with guilt.

"I don't know what I'm doing," Deacon finally admitted, and in that moment Rafe's expression changed from mutinous and determined to one of compassion. Deacon was lost, here, and Rafe was the strong one.

"We're doing this. The interview, spreading the word, antagonizing Felix, getting him to come here," Rafe began. "You'll watch out for me, Mac will be here, and all of us together...no one can beat that. No one else has to die."

Deacon reached out and traced a finger down Rafe's face from his cheekbone to his chin, then pressed to tip his face up a little more.

"What if something happens to you?"

Rafe shook his head. "You won't let it."

Deacon's heart beat faster, his chest tightened, and he knew he would die for this man.

He just had to make sure nothing happened to Rafe in the process. Right now, all he wanted was to kiss Rafe. He cradled Rafe's face, tilted his head and kissed him deeply, and Rafe tangled his hands in Rafe's hair, holding on tight.

"How's the leg? Are you okay?" Deacon asked. Because, hell, nothing else was making a whole lot of sense in his head at the moment. He was there to look after Rafe, not take advantage of the man when he was down.

Rafe shook his head, then quirked a smile. "We're really talking about my leg? Now?"

"What about your scar?"

"Deacon, fuck's sake, man. Take me back to bed."

Deacon bit his tongue, then shrugged in reply and walked them backward into the bedroom. He closed the door and leaned back against it, watching as Rafe awkwardly backed away from him on his crutch until his leg hit the bed. Very slowly and deliberately, he dropped the crutch and shifted his weight so the bed supported him, then he removed his sweats.

But not in one go. Nope. This was all slow and careful, and he was slipping the material from his hips an inch at a time, until all Deacon wanted to do was step forward, shove him onto the bed, and help him.

"What do you want me to do?" he asked, cautiously, in case he broke the spell that Rafe was weaving in this room. *How can I make this better? How can I make you see that I don't want to lose you?*

Rafe didn't answer. He hooked his fingers into his boxers and pushed the material low enough that Deacon got the first real look that wasn't medically related at Rafe's groin. The tease of hair, the V of his hips, and his soft belly were there for Deacon to stare at, and then when he thought that was as far as Rafe would go, the material slid down his legs and only briefly caught on his cast. He shimmied out of them as gracefully as he could, and Deacon stepped forward to help, but Rafe gestured him back with a wave of his hand.

Was this Rafe's attempt at some kind of life-affirming sex? Should Deacon be thinking this through with him?

Crossing his hands over himself, Rafe grasped the hem of his T-shirt and lifted it up and over his head, exposing the warm, toned flesh and cinnamon nipples that were the stuff of Deacon's fantasies. He tossed the T-shirt to the floor, then held out his hands to his sides.

"And?" he asked, and God knew what he was waiting for. Was Deacon expected to say something at this point? Wax lyrical over Rafe, when he was blinded by lust and pain and fear?

"Your wound looks better, less red," Deacon managed, and looked pointedly at the puffiness around the scar, which Rafe had left uncovered.

"Deacon," Rafe growled a warning.

He really wanted this now? With his leg in plaster and his operation scar looking as it might hurt, and with the specter of Felix in the room with them? He wanted Deacon?

"I don't have anything with me," he said, a little helplessly, even though he was harder than fucking iron and he wanted to be right over there with Rafe, kissing him, and sucking him down, and fucking him into tomorrow.

Because clearly I've lost all sense of respect.

"I have it, here."

Oh shit, this just gets worse. Make everything easy.

"Condoms. Lube. I got them from Mac and Sam's room." Rafe pointed at the things on the bed, the familiar packages that Deacon hadn't even noticed.

Some detective you are, he thought. *Were,* he amended.

Just the sight of that and a naked, aroused Rafe had Deacon losing what little control he had left, although he had the presence of mind to make sure the door was closed. Then he unbuckled his belt, unbuttoned his jeans, crossed to Rafe, and pulled him carefully in for a kiss. Rafe was warm and smooth and just the right height and size and everything that Deacon wanted at that moment.

Together, they pulled at Deacon's shirt until Deacon himself popped a few buttons just to get the damn thing off. Rafe attempted to get at his jeans, but Deacon was so hard that he was the only one who would be able to pull them off and not get his erection caught. He toed off his socks, pushed down his jeans, and with them around his thighs he couldn't wait any longer to have Rafe against him, and he yanked a little too hard.

Admittedly, Rafe didn't yelp, but then they were kissing, and any pain would be masked by the slide of tongues frantically twisting in a desperate kiss.

"Tell me," Deacon ordered, "if it hurts."

"You'd better not stop—"

"Rafe—"

"I'm not a delicate freaking flower."

"Okay." Deacon had said his bit and Rafe wasn't listening. "We can find other ways—"

Rafe cut off the explanation, deepening the kiss, then pushed at Deacon's jeans.

"All off." He had demands of his own.

Finally, blissfully, naked, they tumbled back on the bed – or at least Deacon did, and he gently took Rafe with him until Rafe was sprawled over him, just like at the lake. Sense memory of the first time they'd kissed flooded Deacon, and he closed his eyes to the depth of it.

"You have to tell me," he murmured.

"What?" Rafe asked into a kiss.

"If I hurt you, then you have to tell me." Deacon reached up and carded his fingers through Rafe's short hair. "This used to be longer." He was speaking his thoughts out loud, didn't expect an answer, but got one anyway.

"Part of the new me – all grown up, short hair, teacher and respectable townsperson of White Hill, Maine."

Deacon wanted to ask him so much about the town, about his new life, about Felix, but he couldn't, because Rafe looked so needy, leaning over him and kissing his chest. When Rafe bit gently at his nipple, sucking on it, all thoughts of talking fled completely.

Deacon stroked his head and arched up into the touch, sliding his hands down until they rested on Rafe's lower back, letting them lie still and enjoying the attention.

"Come here," he said finally, and tugged at Rafe's arm, wanting kisses, but then more. He kept tugging, inhaling as the weight of Rafe's erection brushed his own.

It took everything in him not to grind up against Rafe and get them off like that.

"Further up," he encouraged, until Rafe moved higher, and with a pillow under his head, Deacon could finally get a taste of Rafe. The access was awkward, the angle off, but it didn't matter, and as soon as he circled Rafe's cock with his lips, Rafe moved up and angled himself just right. Deacon had never quite managed deep-throating, but he'd happily lose the ability to breathe when he could see the expressions passing over Rafe's face. He sucked and licked and moved his hands to cradle Rafe's ass, guiding him, until Rafe jerked away.

"I don't want to…" he murmured. "You inside."

The words were jumbled, but the actions spoke for themselves when he reached for the lube, popped the lid, and squirted way too much onto his hands. Deacon saw frustration and then relief when Rafe reached behind himself and…fuck…he was opening himself up, pushing in lube, and Deacon was trapped under him.

"Rafe, jeez." Blindly, he felt around for condoms, rolling one on as Rafe closed his eyes and pressed back on his fingers. His movements were becoming messy, uncoordinated, his cock against Deacon's thigh, and Deacon lost it completely. He'd wanted to take his time with Rafe, suck him off, stretch him, but fuck if this wasn't the hottest thing he'd ever seen.

"Ready?" Rafe asked, his voice broken.

Deacon didn't have to answer. He held his cock as Rafe slid down, and they stopped momentarily, Rafe's eyes shut in concentration. Then he rested his entire weight on Deacon, and Deacon was in heaven.

Rafe opened his eyes and looked down at Deacon, then smiled; a small, secretive smile with an added wink. "In your own time," he said.

And Deacon laughed.

He couldn't remember the last time he'd laughed during sex, but there was something about this man that pulled him through the whole spectrum of emotions, from anger and fear right through to lust and love. Although he refused to think about that last one too hard.

"Hold on," he said, and tilted his head back a little to indicate the headboard. Rafe got with the plan, wincing once as he moved and reminding Deacon not to do what he really wanted to do. This needed to be all about soft and careful, and he moved slowly, bracing Rafe's hips and careful of his leg, and with mutual sighs they moved together. With every push up, Rafe moved down, circling his hips, waiting a few seconds before letting Deacon lift him up, and he was heavy-lidded, his mouth open, moaning softly at each grind.

"I'm close," he said.

"Touch yourself," Deacon ordered. Then he softened it a little. "Get yourself off, please."

Rafe removed one hand from the headboard and, unbalanced, his eyes widened before he realized Deacon had him steady. Then he circled his cock and began to run his hand up the length, slowly, pressing against the tip, pushing, groaning, his eyes closing, then running his fingers down to where Deacon was fucking up into him. Deacon knew that was game over, feeling his touch where they were joined, and he sped up a little, still taking care but becoming uncoordinated.

"Open your eyes, Rafe."

He opened them, and shuddered as he was coming, and with no words spoken Deacon fell over the edge, his orgasm slamming into him and Rafe arching back.

Rafe was the one who came back down to Earth first, so practical, dealing with the condom and then sliding to Deacon's side, awkwardly and cursing a little.

Deacon drew him close.

"What hurts?" he asked.

"Nothing."

"Don't lie to me."

Rafe looked up at him, and he had the most beautiful hazel eyes. They were sparkling with humor.

"Mostly everything," he admitted.

"I'll get you some meds." Deacon started to move away, but Rafe clung like a spider monkey.

"In a minute," he said, and yawned. "Nap first."

He slept, and Deacon lay awake for every moment of it, his thoughts spiraling from ecstasy to agony and everything in between. He doubted, he talked himself out of the doubts, and then he came to a decision. They weren't doing this thing where Rafe put himself in danger. He would hide Rafe somewhere and he and Mac would go into the city and track Felix down and kill him themselves.

No way was he letting Rafe get hurt.

He watched Rafe wake up, the instinctive stretch, turning in his arms and snuggling in close, that soft moment before he grew into realization of where he was and what was happening. Rafe buried his face in Deacon's throat. He'd said he was willing to put himself in danger to stop others being hurt, but the bravado wasn't there in these first few moments of waking.

"Fuck," he murmured, gripping Deacon tightly. "Fuck, fuck, fuck."

Then he cried.

CHAPTER 13

"D? You in there?"

Mac's voice, and Rafe saw the moment when Deacon became the trained cop, like a shutter came down in an instant. Mac was back and ready to plan whatever they needed to do to get Felix here.

"I'll see you in the kitchen," Deacon called to Mac.

He eased Rafe away and slid out of bed, pulling on his jeans and tee.

"You okay?" he murmured. Rafe nodded, eased off the bed, dressed and picked up his crutch. They heard Mac's retreating steps.

"You think he has a plan for us now?" Rafe asked, unable to keep the fear out of his tone.

"I don't want you doing it."

"I know, but I have to – you know that."

Deacon's tight expression was enough for Rafe to see exactly how he felt about all of this, not that he didn't know that anyway. Deacon went out first and Rafe followed, both of them going into the kitchen and finding a very serious-looking Mac leaning against the counter, his arms crossed over his chest. He didn't hang around in what he had to say.

"He's dead. They found his body in a burned-out car."

Rafe's leg's buckled, and he reached for Deacon to steady himself.

"Jesus Christ, Mac, don't just throw that at him," Deacon snapped, but Rafe held up a hand.

"Really?" he asked.

"They're waiting on dental records, but he was under observation and they're sure it was Felix Martinez in the car."

"So it's done? It's finished?"

Mac nodded. "Yes."

"I think I need a drink," Rafe murmured. He didn't know who passed him a Coke. That wasn't the kind of drink he was talking about, but then the meds wouldn't go well with an entire bottle of vodka, and it was only eight a.m. He sipped it as Deacon and Mac talked about forensics and checks, but he didn't care what they needed to do to check anything. The danger had passed, the man who had got out and who could well have tried to kill him was dead.

How was he supposed to be feeling?

Not numb. Surely he should be happy, relieved; everything was done now. He didn't need to put his life in danger, Felix was dead…hell, Deacon didn't need to look out for him anymore.

Deacon could go back to his own life, and the danger that had thrown them together was over.

"I'm going home," he said, softly at first, and then when neither man in the kitchen reacted to him, he raised his voice. "I'm going home."

"No you're not," Deacon said. "You're not well, and until I see forensic proof that it was Felix in that car—"

"I'm going home." Determined, Rafe stood up and stepped toward the Deacon/Mac wall. He stopped with inches between them. "Let me through to get my stuff."

Given that his stuff consisted of borrowed clothes and a razor, it wouldn't take him long to pack. He just needed to cut this off now. No point in prolonging the misery while Deacon found reasons their infant relationship should stop now. Because, let's face it, this was just sex, and it was sex born of fear. Didn't matter that Rafe had fallen for him all over again; he wasn't forcing Deacon to stay around him any longer than he needed to.

Deacon looked torn, and it was Mac who stepped aside and let Rafe through. Rafe made it all the way to his room before he was stopped by a determined Deacon overtaking him and leaning back against the handle.

"Wait," he said.

"I'm leaving. It's okay, you don't have to worry anymore."

"You're not going anywhere," Deacon said, "because no one will take you." He seemed almost triumphant at the thought that Rafe was stuck there, and that got Rafe's back up. Why would Deacon want him still there when there was no reason?

"Mac will take me," Rafe said, and pointed at Mac, who was hovering by the door. He looked as torn as Deacon. "I'll pay him or something."

"Please, Rafe, think about this. You can rest here, stay just for a while, until the weekend."

"I'm not your problem anymore."

"We made a promise," Deacon said, and moved nearer to Rafe, pulling him close. "Let's just stay until Saturday."

Why was Deacon holding him? Rafe stiffened in the hold and eased away, and a confused-looking Deacon let him go.

"Rafe?"

Rafe couldn't look at him or Mac, slipped into his room and shut the door, hoping that Deacon wouldn't follow him in. People had died. Felix was dead, his parents were gone, and the weight of it – the sheer enormity of what had happened – hit him like a sledgehammer. Running back home wouldn't stop the way he felt.

The first thing he found was his crutch, and he threw it so hard it crashed into the wall. He picked it up, nearly losing his balance, then beat the mattress with it, over and over, cursing and shouting and crying until there was nothing left. He felt Deacon, then, taking the crutch away, easing him back onto the bed, sitting next to him, holding him.

But the acid that burned away inside him didn't stop.

"It's my fault. If I hadn't been at the house, you could have stopped them earlier, you could have caught Felix before this, but you had to watch me, and he was killing, and I fucked up." The words just tumbled out in a mess of nothing at all, and Deacon remained quiet.

Then, "Felix was born a killer," Deacon said into his hair, hugging him from behind. "Doesn't matter if you were at the house or not; he liked to kill. You can't blame yourself for a psychopath's actions."

None of it made Rafe feel any better, because his thoughts were all over the place, and his leg hurt, and his side ached, and he was so fucking done with everything.

He must have fallen asleep, because he never heard Deacon leave, and the clock showed it was midafternoon. He fought disappointment, but then he was the one driving a wedge into whatever they had so that Deacon would feel okay to walk away. Right?

Why would Deacon stay with me anyway?

CHAPTER 14

Things went from bad to worse. Deacon wanted Rafe to stay, but Rafe wanted to go. He shied away every time Deacon went to touch him, and shut himself in his room for the best part of Thursday and Friday.

He was fixated on a single point, that moment when he'd walked into his uncle's house, kept repeating that if he hadn't been there, then Deacon could have got to Felix, Chumo and Arlo earlier. Then Felix wouldn't have killed anyone. The logic was so flawed, but Rafe wasn't listening. Breaking point came when Rafe wouldn't even let Deacon cook him dinner on the Friday evening.

"You don't need to cook me anything."

"It's no bother," Deacon said, and pulled out the pasta and meat.

"No, I don't want you to. I'm going home tomorrow."

"I'm cooking for myself."

Rafe cursed under his breath. "Doesn't mean you need to cook for me. We're done here."

That was when Deacon lost it, big time. He'd been trying to talk, to hug, to kiss, to reassure, and all Rafe wanted was silence and alone time.

"What the fuck is wrong with you? Just because I won't take you home you're sulking like a child who doesn't get what he wants for Christmas!" Deacon wished he could have pulled the words back as soon as he'd said them.

Rafe scrambled to stand, awkwardly with his leg, bracing himself on the wall. "Fuck you, Deacon, just…fuck you."

Then he hobbled out of the hallway and through the door to the bedroom, slamming the door behind him. Deacon knew he'd handled that horribly; he'd just wanted to say something that would ease the pain in Rafe's eyes, and had made it worse. He knew that he saw things in black and white, but this was different – this was all the colors in between, and Rafe was suffering from it. He stood and brushed at his pants, anything to delay the inevitable, then opened Rafe's door.

"I'm sorry," he said from the doorway before Rafe could tell him to go fuck himself again. Rafe was on his bed, sitting on the side, hunched over. All Deacon wanted to do was go over and hug him, try to make him feel better, but his form of comfort wasn't cutting it in this situation.

"I think you need to leave me alone," Rafe said tiredly. "It's okay."

"It's not okay, I thought we had…something."

"You don't have to worry anymore."

"I don't understand this. What happened?"

"Proximity," Rafe mumbled. "I got way too close too fast and forgot who I was. You don't have to worry about me anymore. You didn't want me before – proximity pushed us together, and now we're done."

Deacon couldn't believe what he was hearing. Cautiously, he moved closer. "You think just because Felix is dead that I want to draw a line under what we had going?"

Rafe threw him a quick look. "It was just sex."

Deacon shook his head. "No, it was more than that back when we first met, and it's more than that now."

Hope flickered in Rafe's expression, and Deacon forged ahead with more. "I didn't sleep with you because you were here. I did it because I can't imagine a life where I don't get to touch you, or think about you, or just know that you're mine."

Deacon let out the breath he'd been holding to say all that and crouched in front of him.

"I want more," Rafe said. "I'm not sure I deserve it… I don't…" He stopped and closed his eyes.

"What do you mean?"

"All those people dead. I should never have gone to that house."

"I killed a man," Deacon murmured, the story inside him welling up from the dark place he'd hidden it. He moved to sit next to Rafe, not touching him but close enough that he felt as if he could share the secret quietly. "A year back, I was at a gas station that was being held up. I had a gun, he saw it and he took a hostage, used her as a human shield. She was terrified. I shot him between the eyes, right over her head. The department designated it a clean shot, but I never got my head around that one thing; what if I'd not been armed? He would have taken what he wanted and left us all alive. He just wanted money. He didn't want to die."

Rafe unclenched his fists on the quilt and moved one of them closer to Deacon, nearly close enough to touch but not quite. Deacon wanted to take his hand, but he didn't want pity, he just wanted to explain.

"So I quit."

"You were doing your job."

"That wasn't what made me quit. There was an internal review and I was taken off active cases for two months, and in those two months other people were hurt, or died. Drugs made their way onto the streets, and I felt responsible for it all. I took that all on me, everything going back to that single moment when Edgar Mackie wanted money and responded to seeing me armed."

"You felt as if you had to save everyone?"

"Yeah, and it took me a while to get my head out of that spiral. You'll find your way out of this one day."

"I wanted to find evidence that my uncle killed my mom, and then my dad. That was all I wanted; not justice for everyone in the entire world."

Deacon thought they were talking at cross-purposes, and he debated telling Rafe about the people he'd saved after the family had trusted him, after he'd shot Rafe and gained their twisted respect. Maybe he'd save that for another day.

"I'm tired," Rafe said quietly, and bumped shoulders with Deacon.

"There's something I want to ask you," Deacon said into the quiet of the room.

"Uh-huh?" He wasn't listening now, he was more than done with everything.

"I'd like you to have a tracker on you."

"Uh-huh."

"Rafe, are you listening to me?"

Deacon sounded stressed, and Rafe looked up to Deacon holding something out to him. A small black disc.

"Put it in your pocket, just in case."

Rafe took it, but stared at it, not quite knowing what to say. "Why?" he asked.

Deacon shrugged. "Humor me?"

Rafe nodded, he could do that. He slipped it in the pocket of the jacket he'd borrowed from Sam. No point in putting it in his jeans; nothing was going to happen to him here with Deacon next to him. Anyway, Sam had said he could keep it, and he liked it, so decided he would. He'd wear it anytime he wasn't with Deacon, problem solved.

Seemingly happy with that, Deacon scooted back to rest on the pillows, and pulled Rafe back with him until they were spooning on top of the quilt. Maybe they should have rethought that, got undressed and under the covers? There was a blanket at the base of the bed, and Deacon hooked it with a foot and pulled it over them.

Rafe pushed back into him, wriggled a little to get comfy, but there was nothing sexual about it. Rafe needed a hug, Deacon needed to hug him, and together like that, they slept.

CHAPTER 15

All Rafe could think about in the car was whether Deacon was scared.

From Sam and Mac's place to the small town of Cambridge Falls was only a morning's drive, even though they had to cross two state lines to get to it, blink and you'd miss it through New Hampshire, then just over the state line into Maine. The journey was quiet and flew by, not much talking from either of them, but, yeah, the whole concept of a scared Deacon was something that Rafe couldn't shake.

"Are you ever scared?" he asked when they were little more than twenty minutes or so from Rafe's small house on Main in the town.

"Of you getting hurt, yes," Deacon answered without any real thought.

Rafe had nothing else to say, and let Deacon concentrate on driving. This northeast corner of the US was beautiful in Fall; a blanket of gold and red swept as far as the eye could see, and lush grass carpeted the ground. When he'd been asked where he wanted to go, when he'd been given a choice, he'd remembered the conversation with Deacon at the lake and said Massachusetts.

They hadn't outright laughed at his choice, but Maine had been as close as they could get.

"You knew where I was put in WitSec, didn't you?" He'd meant to ask that before, or state it as fact.

"Not exactly, but Evie kept tabs on you, and every so often she'd tell me everything was okay, until it wasn't."

Silence again.

They stopped at a diner with a little over ten miles to go to Cambridge Falls, a small, out-of-the-way place that had seen better days. Deacon opened the door and gestured for Rafe to enter first, then he chose a table in the corner by the exit with his back to the wall. Rafe wasn't ready to have his back to anything, and he wriggled into the other seat. Then he imagined having to make a quick exit with his leg in plaster, wedged in so tight, and panic snagged in his chest. He began to move to get out, but Deacon laid a hand over his.

"Sorry," he murmured. "Force of habit."

"You're freaking me out," Rafe said under his breath. He tried to get out again, but this time Deacon's touch was firmer.

Rafe relaxed a little as the waitress made her way over with mugs and a jug of hot coffee.

"Coffee?" she asked, and filled both mugs when Rafe nodded and Deacon gave a low yes. The outside of the diner looked dated, but the service was quick and friendly, and the coffee hot. "What can I get you?"

"Pancakes, bacon, eggs," Deacon said, "and toast."

The waitress looked at Rafe expectantly. "Toast," he said, to placate her and to rid Deacon of the worried frown. Sue him, but he wasn't hungry at all.

She took the order, bustled back with a basket of condiments and jellies, and left.

The toast arrived, and the scent of it was enough to have Rafe buttering it and adding jelly, but then he stared at it, even as Deacon ate his huge plate of food. Not even the scent of bacon was working for him.

Rafe bit a piece of toast and chewed it thoughtfully. It tasted pretty good, and he felt a little hungry. Maybe it was because he was getting closer to home that he was so nervous. He finished the toast, washed it down with coffee, and waited for Deacon to finish.

Abruptly, he wanted to see his place, his home, and he wanted to show it to Deacon.

"I can't wait for you to see Cambridge Falls," he said as they rose to leave. Deacon threw down some money to cover the check and held open the door to let Rafe out first. "I feel like the only thanks I can give you for all this is for you to see me back home safe where I belong," he added as soon as they were out in the chilly Fall air.

Deacon shrugged into his jacket and gently patted Rafe on the chest. "You don't ever have to thank me, but I can't wait to see your town and your place."

They were back on the road within seconds, and the general feeling of wellbeing that Rafe had felt disappeared quicker than ice in the sun when Deacon swore with feeling.

Deacon slowed up and indicated. "Seems like we've got company," he said.

Fear gripped Rafe as he twisted in his seat to look behind them. "Who is it?" How long would it be before fear wasn't his constant companion?

"Local PD."

Rafe didn't feel much less concerned by the news. Cops meant questions.

"Let me handle this," Rafe said, and Deacon didn't answer, although he lowered his window and had his documents to hand.

A man Rafe recognized leaned down to the car. "License and registration, sir."

"Bill, hey," Rafe said, like it hadn't been a while since he'd been in town and the last time he'd been there he hadn't been driven away in an ambulance.

"Craig," Bill said in surprise, and rested his hands on the roof of the car, peering in. "That you?" It was weird to hear his fake name. Both he and Deacon would have to be careful to use it when they were in town.

"Sure is," Rafe said, not letting one iota of his worry into his tone, and slipping back into his witness program name easily.

"Heard you left the city hospital AMA. We were all kinda worried."

"You know how it is," Rafe said, thinking on his feet. Deacon shot him a look that spoke volumes. *You know how it is, what?*

"How you doing?"

"Better, thank you. Bill, meet my friend Deacon."

Bill extended a hand. "Welcome to Cambridge Falls."

"Sir," Deacon replied, and shook his hand. He was formal and polite, but Rafe could see the tension radiating from him. Surely that was something that Bill would pick up on.

"You boys drive carefully now." Bill puffed himself up importantly, "See you at the town meeting tomorrow at the school. Bring your *friend.*"

"I'll be there."

"Good to have you back, Craig."

"Good to be back."

Pleasantries exchanged, Bill returned to his car, waving as he drew out and passed them.

Was it just Rafe, or had there been an emphasis on the word *friend,* and a sly wink from the crusty old cop? Everyone in town knew he was gay. He'd told the school principal at his interview, and it seemed like by the first day on the job everyone had known he wasn't interested in Betsy's cousin Katie, and would probably prefer her other cousin, Tad.

When they got into the small town, Rafe felt as if he'd been away forever, when in reality it hadn't been long at all.

"We're here," Deacon said, and slowed up for the one set of stoplights.

Rafe glanced up and realized where they were. To the left led to his house, to the right took you to the school where he taught

Rafe's apartment was over a bakery, Carter's, and sandwiched between a diner and a grocery store. Seems as Deacon knew exactly where he lived. Of course he did.

"This is home," he said needlessly, and waited as Deacon pulled up farther along the road and killed the engine. Deacon helped him out of the car, and together they managed the iron steps up the side of the café to his front door.

Nothing had changed, the door was still red, but things should have changed. He'd been away for a while now, not been back since the hit-and-run had put him in the hospital. He didn't have a key, it wasn't as if Deacon took any personal belongings from the hospital along with Rafe. Still, Deacon managed to get inside with a collection of keys on a ring. The smell inside was better than he would have imagined. A couple of the plants he'd been nurturing were long since dead – no one else had a key to his place, part of his WitSec agreement. Mail had piled up at the door, a lot of it junk mail, some bills, but utilities were all paid monthly direct, so he knew there wouldn't be any letters demanding money. Hell, he didn't even have a credit card. Craig Jenkins lived within his means and didn't draw any attention to himself, until of course he did with the article. So stupid.

"Nice place," Deacon said, and closed the front door behind him. He looked so big in this place, but he looked right, as if he fit into Rafe's idea of home. The drapes were open, just as he'd left them to go to work that morning, and his small kitchen still tidy, his bed made. He knew his DVR would be full of recorded shows from his favorite Discovery Channel.

Nothing had changed.

Just him.

First thing he did was flick on the hot water; he needed a shower. Then he thought about what Deacon might need, and set about making coffee. And through all of this he didn't say a word, and Deacon just watched him.

"You okay?" he finally asked.

Rafe wasn't sure where to start; this place was more his home than any he'd had since his dad had died. He felt secure here, safe, and he loved this town, and his job. In fact, what he wanted to do was smile, so he did. Deacon tugged him close and they kissed, right in the middle of the tiny sitting room.

Now all Rafe had to do was convince Deacon that this could be his home as well.

Where did that thought come from?

But Rafe knew where it had originated. Right from inside his heart.

CHAPTER 16

In his house, with the door shut and Deacon making breakfast, Rafe could almost forget that tomorrow he was going back to work. They'd made love last night, slow and gentle, and afterward they'd laid for the longest time, just talking. Deacon told him all about being a cop, Rafe explained how much he loved teaching.

They were like a normal, everyday kind of couple.

"How do you want your eggs?" Deacon asked, pulling him from his memories of the previous night.

"Scrambled. Thanks."

The conversation was that simple, and when they sat next to each other on the sofa, plates piled high with eggs and bacon, Rafe wished he could capture this moment forever. Soon Deacon would have to leave to go back to real life. Didn't matter how much Rafe wanted him to stay and make something of what they were, he would have to go. Rafe was going to miss him. Or at least miss the sex. That was what it was—just the sex.

Who was he kidding? Deacon leaving wouldn't be good.

"Why did you stop being a cop?" He asked the question that had been bugging him for a while. When they'd first met, Deacon had been undercover. Now he wasn't anything, and in his words it had been a few months since he'd resigned.

"I already told you."

"Yeah, you said about the shooting, but you were doing your job, right? A career you were good at. Why would you leave? Couldn't you get support, help to keep on working?"

Deacon swallowed the mouthful of bacon and scooped up some eggs, chewing and swallowing them as well. He did everything deliberately and slowly, and Rafe wondered if he was ever getting a real answer.

"Honestly, I was already on the edge after being undercover. I'd lost part of my identity doing that." He stopped, ate some more, and Rafe didn't interject with any more questions. He knew Deacon wasn't done yet.

Deacon looked at Rafe. "When we took Arlo in, and his sons, I'd done my job, you know?"

"Yeah," Rafe murmured.

"But shooting you, and watching you afterward, when you struggled at first with what had happened—"

"Wait, you watched me?"

"No, that sounds like…no, I wasn't watching you, but I knew where you were, and Evie kept me in the loop as to how you were doing. The town was a good match when you got here, but before you settled here, I know you were left with a lot of questions."

Rafe put his plate on the small table, turning to face Deacon. "Like how was it the man I saw with compassion in his eyes had to kill me? That was my biggest question back then. The answer you gave me, about the others that died, and how you wanted to protect me? I get that. I understand that."

Deacon put his plate on the table and sat back on the sofa, cupping his coffee. His hazel eyes darkened, and he half closed his eyes in thought. "Some of the things I saw…" he began slowly. "You'd put yourself right in the middle of it all, and I was growing to care about you. I wasn't just guarding you, I was falling for you, and I saw vulnerability and a good heart, not blackness and poison. I didn't want to shoot you, and right after we arrested Arlo and his sons, I wanted to wake you up in the hospital and tell you everything. But I couldn't."

Rafe scooted forward a bit, just needing to touch some part of Deacon. He had just as much that he needed to get off his chest.

Deacon leaned into him, and Rafe pressed back, and like that they slipped into an easy silence. He was going back to work in the morning, and after a while lost to sitting on the sofa, he pulled himself together and sat at the small kitchen table. He lost himself in coloring in and laminating all kinds of things to do with the letters B and C for his five-year-olds tomorrow.

Deacon came to sit with him, and without prompting he sat there and cut out letters, placing them in a neat pile. He didn't complain even though there were fifteen of each letter, not to mention fifteen bears and fifteen cats.

"What made you want to teach the little kids?" Deacon asked, frowning when he couldn't get a proper hold of the tiny scissors they were using.

"I didn't have a lot of choice. It was the only vacancy, and I'd done early years as an elective at college. Two weeks of intense training, and I joined the school as Mr. Jenkins, teacher to a class of five-year-olds."

"Do you enjoy it?"

Rafe nodded. "It's important to me."

Silence for a while, but when Rafe finished cutting out the last B, he sighed and realized he had one hell of a lot of questions.

"I'm not in normal WitSec, am I? Not as when the government knows where I am. I mean, there was no need for me still to be in Cambridge Falls. Arlo was dead, Chumo as well, and Felix in a psychiatric hospital. My part was done. Right? Any typical person would have been back to their normal life."

Deacon put down his laminated teddy bear and unhooked the scissors, flexing his fingers. "You had to stay dead until I thought it was safe. If Felix had ever realized…"

"Which he did."

"He was ranting about you being the murderer, about how without you everything was okay. He blamed you. But you were okay; you were dead and out of his way. I didn't have to worry."

"Okay." Rafe went back to cutting, but Deacon clearly had something else he wanted to say, because he didn't pick up the scissors.

"But yeah, the WitSec you were in wasn't sanctioned. With all three of the Martinez family away, I couldn't swing getting you protection, not officially anyway. So I pulled some strings and we got you here. Can I ask you something, though?"

"Sure."

"Are you happy here? Is this the life you'd want if you could choose it?"

That was an easy question to answer. "I love this town, the apple Danish and coffee in the morning, the hellos you get from everyone, the love of the kids, the school and my work colleagues. I have friends. I would never have looked at teaching as a career, but I love it. I just wish I hadn't made such a fuss about the LGTB group, otherwise I wouldn't have been in the paper and Felix may never have seen it."

"Rafe—"

"But then I would always have been thinking, why did Deacon hurt me, and where was Felix, and were more people dying because of that family?"

Deacon looked down at the pile of teddies and shuffled them with his hands. They looked so tiny against his fingers, and Rafe could only imagine what was going through Deacon's head at that moment.

"I wouldn't have let him hurt you in that hit-and-run if I could have got to you first," he said finally. He sounded so serious, so focused and determined, that for the first time in the last few weeks, Rafe felt completely safe.

"Thank you," he said, and went back to crafts, and for the longest time they sat quietly, the only sound the scissors in the card.

"My teacher in first grade was this really old woman who smelled of peppermint," Deacon cut into the silence with a brand-new subject that wasn't about death and fear. "Probably in hindsight she was thirty, but she seemed old to me when I was five."

"One of the kids in my class wanted to know if I'd met any dinosaurs, so I know they all think I'm old."

Rafe picked up the letters and the bears, placing them in a folder along with some worksheets he'd printed out, and then he was done.

They made dinner together, watched crappy TV, and halfway through a rerun of some godawful soap, Rafe switched off the TV altogether.

"You could go now if you want. No sense in dragging this out if you want to get back to your own life," he blurted into the otherwise silent room. There, he had it off his chest.

He had a hundred reasons in his head for why he'd said what he had, but they were lost when Deacon hauled him in for a hard, desperate kiss.

"I'm not going anywhere."

They stumbled back at the force of the coming-together, but Deacon didn't let him fall. Instead, with heated kisses, he encouraged Rafe backward to the bedroom, assisting him even as they kissed so he didn't fall over his damn cast.

Gently, Deacon laid him on the bed, but there was still fire in his eyes, and the kisses went back to being determined and focused.

"I'm not leaving," he repeated between kisses, and carefully eased Rafe up the bed, not touching the tender area in his side or his leg. He was impossibly gentle, but wouldn't let Rafe move.

How is he even doing that?

"You and me," he whispered, "we've got a long time to figure us out."

"Deacon—"

"Things are not ending tomorrow, or the day after. I want more than this."

They kissed again, and something about the desperation and tenderness made Rafe melt. He forgot his leg ached and his side hurt, and he was finally at peace.

CHAPTER 17

When he woke up at the alarm the next morning, Deacon was gone, but he could hear him on a conference call with various voices, and Rafe wasn't ready to hear anything else about what was happening in Deacon's real life. Not yet. He showered, shaved, and dressed in neat pants, a shirt and tie, and for the longest time he stared at himself in the mirror, wondering if people would notice any change in him when he got to school. Only when he was sure that Rafe Martinez had been pushed back and Craig Jenkins was at the forefront of his thoughts did he leave the bedroom. The conference call was done, Deacon dressed in his usual jeans and a tee shirt.

Rafe wanted another kiss, needed it more than the next breath. He slid his hand up and laid it against Deacon's cheek, looking into his hazel eyes, and then in a smooth move he kissed him. There were no walls to press him against, no chance of friction or more than just a kiss, but all he needed was one taste of Deacon and everything would make sense. At least for a while.

Deacon rested his hands on Rafe's hips and held him close as they kissed – lazy, searching kisses that were everything that Rafe needed right now. When they eased apart, Deacon was smiling that enigmatic half smile that sent shivers down Rafe's spine.

Abruptly, inside him, all the hidden secrets and everything he hadn't felt he could say spilled out in a hurried, blurted, "I love you."

He waited for Deacon's smile to drop, for him to become all business and dismiss his feelings as a link they had because of proximity, or danger, or some other nonsense that Rafe had been thinking himself. Instead Deacon kissed him again, and when they parted it was Deacon's turn to say something.

"I love you too," he murmured. "I'll walk you to school."

One last kiss, and finally they couldn't avoid leaving the apartment any longer.

The colder night air hadn't dissipated much, the bite of winter in the cool breeze that skipped along Main and channeled into the alley that held the entrance to the apartment. The school was a five minutes' walk, ten when he added in getting coffee and a Danish for breakfast.

Why break routine? He needed the stability of the things he usually did, or he'd be a basket case before he got to school.

Johan had his order ready, but there was a delay when Deacon ordered his black coffee and selected his own Danish. Johan nodded and said he'd add that to the normal morning order.

Deacon was his boyfriend, and Johan knew that. So did Anna, who was just going into the grocery store for formula, and several other regular town people who spoke to Rafe. Every time he stopped, Deacon was at his side, sipping his coffee, although the Danish was untouched so far.

The town looked as normal now as it had done that day weeks ago when he'd been walking to school and a car had sped down Main and headed straight for him. The sense memory of the pain when it had hit him had him hesitating at the lights.

"Okay?" Deacon asked.

"The car, the one that hit me. I was remembering."

"What about it? Details?"

"No, I don't even recall the color of it – I just remember it hitting me. I never saw it, or heard it, or knew the driver, didn't matter how much anyone asked. When I woke up in the hospital, all I could think was that I wasn't feeling pain at all. The meds were good." Rafe needed to lighten the explanation. "We don't know for sure it was Felix; I mean, it could have been anyone, and him getting away from the place he was in was just a freaky coincidence."

"It was him," Deacon said without hesitation. "I know that for sure."

And Rafe knew as well.

The school was still the same. The large, sprawling building was home to a range of students, from the little ones to those about to go on to their senior high school years, the typical school that fed many small towns. Rafe loved teaching there, and that had been the most positive thing in his life since WitSec, or whatever he was part of, had decided he needed to be hidden away. Gone were the dreams of being a lawyer, but instead, he was a teacher of the littlest of the kids, and he loved every minute of it.

The teacher's lounge was usually split into three distinct groups of teachers and TAs. The primary school teachers in one corner, the junior high teachers in the other, and in the middle the ones who didn't care and wanted to chat. Today was completely different. Everyone crowded around Rafe, shaking his hand, hugging him, his absence after the "accident" had been noticed and mourned over. He had to get used to being called Craig Jenkins again; he'd got used to being called Rafe by Deacon.

This was like getting back into character, and it was hard, until abruptly he was feeling being Mr. Craig Jenkins, teacher, back from a sabbatical.

"I had to cover the Apples," muttered one of his fellow primary teachers, Oscar Ebson. The Apples were the five-year-olds, a group of fifteen precocious, adventurous, challenging, inquisitive kids. They were Rafe's class, and he wanted them back. "Glad you're here, Jenkins," Oscar added, and held out his fist for a bump.

"Good to be back," Rafe answered, and bumped him back.

The staff room cleared as teachers left for their lessons, and he refilled his coffee before heading for his classroom.

His TA, a young girl called Melissa, was waiting at the door. "Welcome back Mr. J," she said with a grin. "You ready for this?" She gestured to his leg, and he nodded ruefully. It wasn't his leg he was worried about, but the pain in his side.

"Ready as I'll ever be."

"They said they'd be super good for you today, but Billy has already made Michael cry once this morning because he's started ballet lessons and Billy…" She didn't need to say anymore. Billy came from a family that wasn't known for its tolerance, and Michael was a kid who loved art and dancing. The two were either going to kill each other or become best friends. That was what Rafe loved most about the job; seeing the kids change in their first year in school, making it the best he could for them. Hopefully he'd show Michael that dancing and art were good things to love and be good at, and he'd show Billy that he didn't have to be like his older brothers, all five of them, and to be tolerant of differences.

I don't ever want this to stop.

He waited, his hand on the doorknob.

"You okay, Mr. J?"

Rafe nodded. "I'm fine," he said out loud, not letting his doubts seep into his voice. "Let's do this."

He opened the door, and fifteen kids crowded tight around him.

"We did a poster!"

"Why can't we see your cast? Will you take your pants off?"

"Why were you away so long?"

"Did the car hurt when it hit you?"

"My mum says you coulda died, Mr. Jenkins. Is that true?"

He held a hand above his head, and one by the one the class fell silent. "Let's go sit on the mat and I'll tell you everything."

Well, almost everything, at least.

Recess came and went. They'd covered most of the questions, apart from whether or not the car hitting him had hurt. He'd broken up a squabble over Lego, worked on the letter B, and accepted three apples from the kids.

The rest of the morning was uneventful, lunch was quiet, and he saw no sign of Deacon. He wondered what he was doing with himself. Billy was now the one crying – turned out he didn't want to go home – and Michael was the one hugging him, along with Louise, who hugged everyone all the time.

He settled them in for the closing story, opening the giant copy of a brightly colored book featuring a boy and a bear and lots of water. A perennial favorite with all the kids.

Fifteen minutes to end of the day and the kids were flagging, and he made a point of allowing some extra time for packing up their lunchboxes and bags. He always tried to get his class out of the school first so he had time for the parents, so they weren't caught up with the older kids who messed everything up. Melissa was an awesome TA and had them all corralled at the door with ten minutes to spare.

Today had been a good day. Being back here was exactly what he needed.

When he walked out of the school, Deacon was waiting, and Rafe decided he could get used to it.

CHAPTER 18

It was always weird seeing the school at night. Empty of children, with the classrooms in darkness, it always made Rafe uneasy. He loved the school noise, the bright lights and colors, but the hall was the only place in town big enough for the town meeting. He'd missed the last one, but the minutes went from parking to lawns, and he didn't think he'd missed much.

Deacon had insisted on coming as well, and he'd clearly gone shopping somewhere, because he had a new shirt that stretched over each muscle. He'd caught the eye of quite a few of the ladies here tonight, but he was oblivious.

The hall was cold as well, and everyone had to wear coats until the portable heaters kicked in; school cost-cutting meant the thermostat was turned down overnight. Rafe had taken Sam's jacket and only when he pushed his hands into its pockets to warm them did he feel the black disc, the tracker.

To think there had been a time he'd needed that little disc to reassure himself that he'd be okay.

As usual, tables groaned with donated food, and soft drinks, and chatter that escalated in volume as each new person joined. Everyone wanted to talk to Rafe about the accident and wanted to know who Deacon was. Rafe was the one who suggested they'd met at the hospital, and everyone seemed happy with that explanation.

Why wouldn't they be? No one here knew about their connection. People were interested in Deacon only in that they assumed he was Rafe's boyfriend. For a small town, the residents were welcoming, but he still wanted to be circumspect around the parents of the kids he taught. Cambridge Falls School was home to one hundred students pulled from all over the area, aged from five to Junior High. The rest of their education was handled by the large senior high school a few towns over. Everyone knew each other – things didn't get done in this town without consensus, and this appeared to include Rafe's accident. They were debating more stop lights, so Rafe found a chair at the back of the lounge and perched on its arm, Deacon next to him, standing, with his hands in his pockets.

Anna came over, her youngest daughter in her arms. "Can you take her?" she asked Rafe, who held out his arms. He loved the little ones, and Chloe was only eleven months old. In a few years she'd be in his school and he'd be teaching her the alphabet and how to count to ten. He'd seen this baby born, or at least seen her when she was only a few days old, and had watched her blossom from cute-baby to aware-baby, to this point where she was normally desperately trying to escape everyone's hold to crawl around. Only she was asleep now, and Rafe cradled her. He ran a finger softly down her face, right to the little birthmark on her shoulder, a star shape that meant her name had almost been Starlight, which hadn't gone down too well with Anna's husband. So, Chloe she had become.

The meeting was long. There was consensus on another set of lights, and a warning to watch parking outside the school. Like that would have stopped the hit-and-run by an unknown assailant that had nearly taken Rafe out.

Of course, the assailant was known, and all these people spread out in the hall were oblivious to everything. Rafe was friends with a lot of them, passing acquaintances with others, but every single person there was part of this town.

"They need to know," he murmured, and rocked Chloe.

"No, they don't," Deacon said back.

Looking down at the baby in his arms, all Rafe could think was that there was every reason to be honest about everything, but then he wouldn't be Craig Jenkins anymore, he'd be Rafe again, and they would know he was related to the Martinez family. Deacon appeared to pick up on his discomfort, and pressed a hand to Rafe's knee.

"It's okay," he reassured him in a low tone.

Rafe had to believe that was true, even as Chloe curled up and snuffled against his shirt. Any moment she would wake up, and this sweet interlude would be over.

Anna came over and took Chloe from him. "Need to get this little one to bed," she said quietly.

Rafe was bereft when the baby had gone. Without the baby on his chest, he would probably have to mingle, to talk to the people who would ask him all the same questions about his leg, about how he was feeling.

The meeting went on, this time focusing on Christmas and the lighting on Main, and was it possible to fundraise for more, and hey, did anyone have any ideas. By the time another hour had passed, Rafe's leg was aching like a bitch.

"I'm just going to walk this out and visit the bathroom," he said, and tapped his leg.

"I'll come with," Deacon said, and helped him to stand just as the sheriff wandered over their way.

"I'm okay," he murmured. "Give me five."

"Coffee?" Oscar said from the other side of Deacon.

"I'll come back for mine."

He made his way through the crowd of people with plates of food. He could answer the questions about the leg from the few friends in town he'd made – Sheila who owned the café, Johan whose dad owned the grocery store and had just retired, leaving Johan in charge. Ultimately, though, he wanted some air. He used the bathroom and limped back the way he'd come, bypassing someone standing with his back to him.

"Hi," he said in his friendliest tone, and then saw the baby. He didn't have to see the birthmark to know that it was Chloe. He recognized her – the sleepsuit, the blanket, and there was blood. A lot of blood.

Ice froze his heart, and he looked up at the man holding her.

Right into the cold, dead eyes of Felix Martinez. One side of his face was a mess of burns, raw and bleeding, and he was hunched to one side, but he was holding Chloe and he looked determined.

"You don't want me to hurt the baby like I'm hurting the mom, right?" he said, his voice slurry, one side of his mouth split and twisted.

"Felix—"

"Best come with me, huh?"

Felix headed for the door and pushed it open.

"Gray Mazda at the back. Get in the driver's seat."

Rafe was frozen in place. Felix was supposed to be dead, burned in a car. Should he go back out the door and shout for Deacon? What was happening here? Then Chloe whimpered and Rafe's decision was easy.

"Leave the baby here," Rafe pleaded, watching as Felix looked down at Chloe and snarled at her.

"I don't wanna hurt a baby yet, but the mom? She's all kinds of bloody in the trunk. Wanna see?"

"Don't..." Rafe didn't know what to say, how to stop this. He needed Deacon. Where was Deacon? How the hell had he even got into the school? "They'll know you're here," he said.

"Then who's stopping me? 'Cause I don't see anyone armed and heading my way." He popped the trunk, and to Rafe's horror he saw Anna, unconscious, tied up in there.

"Get in the fucking car." When Rafe hesitated, Felix lifted Chloe above his head and grimaced. "Want me to hurt this little thing?"

"Felix, Jesus."

Rafe didn't know what to do. Did he get in the car, where the baby would be out of his reach, or did he try to wrestle the baby away from Felix? Was Anna even alive? Felix slammed the trunk closed before Rafe could focus on checking her breathing.

"Get. In. The. Car."

He still hadn't lowered Chloe, and Rafe began to do as he was told, relief running through him as Felix laid the baby on the back seat. This was his moment – grab Chloe and run.

"I will kill you here and now." Rafe froze at the gun pointing at him. "And then I'll finish this baby's momma, and then maybe I'll leave the baby right next to her bleeding corpse, what do you say?"

"If I go with you, you'll let Anna and her baby go?"

"You have my word," Felix said, then snorted a laugh. "You got no fucking room to negotiate."

He sat in the passenger seat, pulling on his belt. Chloe was lying loose on the back seat, so there was no way that Rafe could crash the car; there was nothing he could do. He started the engine, hoping to God Deacon would appear.

Nothing.

They were on the main road out of town, no roadblock, no police, nothing. The streets were empty this time of night, and not a single law enforcement officer anywhere.

They drove for twenty minutes, out of town and up the windy roads to the base of the mountain, the clock ticking away the seconds, and Chloe woke up and was sobbing in the back, with Felix growing more agitated.

"Jesus, fucking baby. Pull over," Felix ordered, waving the gun in Rafe's face.

"Fuck, no, don't hurt her – I can get her to stop crying."

Chloe was screaming now. "Stop. The. Car."

Rafe did as he was told. He wasn't belted in – he'd put himself between a bullet and baby Chloe if he had to.

"Get her out of the car." Rafe reached to pick up Chloe, and Felix shoved him toward the trunk. "Her, for fuck's sake."

Rafe opened the trunk and got Anna out as quickly as he could, thankful he could still hear Chloe sobbing in the car. At least that meant she was still alive, even if she was distressed.

"Lie her down over there."

Rafe stared into the darkness. They were in the middle of nowhere, not on a main highway, it was cold, and they were abandoning Anna?

"She'll die," Rafe said.

"You think?" Felix laughed again, and shoved him and Anna away from the car. "Over there," he said with a wave of the gun.

Rafe placed Anna carefully on the ground, hoping the rocks she lay against would be enough shelter. She was breathing, although the blood on her face was sticky to touch.

"Get the fucking baby," Felix snapped, and Rafe hurriedly returned and gripped Chloe close. "Take her to her momma." He gestured with the gun, and Rafe went straight to where Anna lay.

"Please Felix, don't hurt them. You have me…"

Felix ignored him. "Put the brat with her momma."

"It's too cold. She'll die."

"Gonna die anyway. Leave her."

Rafe fell to his knees next to Anna. "Wake up, Anna, please." He had no phone, nothing to leave with them, and they were in the middle of nowhere. He placed Chloe next to her mom, in her mom's arms, and inspiration hit him.

He was going to die, but there was no way he was leaving the girls to die as well.

"Craig?" Anna whispered, her focus bleary.

Rafe shrugged out of his jacket and wrapped Chloe in it, snuggling her back with her mom. The tracker would lead Deacon here, to Anna and the baby, and they would be safe.

"Thank you," Anna whispered, her voice stronger.

"Stay alive," Rafe said back. "Tell Deacon…"

"Craig?"

"Tell him I'm sorry."

"Get the fuck over here," Felix snapped from behind them.

Careful to keep himself between the gun and the little family, he walked back to the car, waiting until they were both ready to get back in. If anything happened to Anna or Chloe, it would kill him. He wasn't going to let anyone else die for him.

They drove for another few minutes, and Rafe honestly had no idea where they were going. They'd moved between the mountains, taken a side road, and ended up at a shack. That was all it was – a broken-down shack – but it was obviously where Felix had been staying. There was a camping stove, and a sleeping bag, and chains. A lot of chains.

And bodies. He counted three, laid in a precise line.

Rafe tried to take everything in, so he could tell someone if he managed to live past today. He wanted them to know there was blood here, and the chains were stained with it, and he had no clue whether the blood was from Felix killing, and that he was terrified about what would happen next.

Terrified but resigned.

"On your knees," Felix said, his voice soft, the gun right in Rafe's face.

This was it; the moment when he was going to die. Rafe went to his knees on the dark, damp ground, the give of it making him think there was earth there, and no floor to this place. "Hands out in front of you."

With practiced ease, one-handed, Felix slipped loose rope around Rafe's wrists, then with one tug he tightened it before moving behind him.

"Hands over your head," he said, and Rafe felt the press of cold steel to the nape of his neck. He'd felt a gun against him before, only that time Deacon had saved him.

Felix grabbed his tied hands and hooked them to something, and then slowly he walked to face Rafe head on and pulled on a chain. As he did so, Rafe was pulled to his feet and then higher, until only the tips of the feet of his good leg were on the ground, just enough to balance him with his arms at full stretch. His cast made him lopsided, and he knew he should care that his side hurt, but he couldn't.

"You should have died when I hit you with the car," Felix said, in a sing-song voice as if he was telling a story. "But your daddy didn't die either. I drove that car straight at him – thirty, forty, fifty miles an hour. He shoulda died when he hit the windshield, but no, the fucker held on for fucking days."

"I'll kill you," Rafe snapped, and tried to pull on the chains.

"You, I went slower, 'cause I wanted you in pain for what you did to us. Then I was going to kill you in the hospital, suffocate you, watch you squirm. You left. Now I get to kill you as I wanted all along. Slowly and painfully."

Felix smiled, then, placing the gun very deliberately on the floor, and Rafe took his chance, kicking out at Felix and catching him in his side. It wasn't enough to make any difference, and all Felix did was jump back and laugh at Rafe.

"You know what my dad said? He had to kill your mom, course he did, but he told me his sister was feisty when he killed her. She refused to die, even when he hit her over and over, and you know what he said after that?"

Felix poked Rafe in the side, then the chest. Hard.

"Dad told me she said she was ready to make a bargain. Anything to keep you alive. He told me he shoulda killed you the same day. Fucking spawn of something so perfect and your street rat dad." Felix's words were getting more incoherent as he spoke.

"Fuck you," Rafe snarled, anger and despair kicking his fear down to levels he could handle.

Rafe kicked out again; he wasn't listening and he wasn't going to answer.

"I don't want you to fuck me," Felix said, and ran a hand from Rafe's chin to his waist and then deliberately punched him in the groin. "That diseased cock is getting nowhere near me."

Felix disappeared into the darkness of this shed. Then he laughed, but there was no joy in it.

The hit, when it came, was right across Rafe's back, a path of fire that stole his breath. A second hit, and he heard the rip as his shirt caught on whatever Rafe was hitting him with.

"I'll be with Dad soon, you know. They'll get me soon enough, but not before I take you as well. Someone pushed a shiv in Chumo's side. My beautiful brother, dying as he bled out alone in his cell. And Dad? He heard Chumo was dead, and he had a heart attack; having to stand in front of a judge, you know, that started to kill him a day at a time, and it was all because of you and your cop friend. You did that to him. We were fine until you arrived. You." Another hit, and this time Rafe couldn't help the shout of pain. "Blood," Felix said, and disappeared again. "Had a guy in the city, wanted him to bleed, but he died way too quickly. I like to take my time. Dad always said I was the best at making the pain last. That old guy was a disappointment. And as for the others… I give up on making things last anymore."

"You're fucked in the head," Rafe said.

A fist came out of the darkness and caught him under his left eye, stole his breath and any sense of where he was.

Rafe knew he was in bad shape, wished Felix would just kill him. He thought it had been forever – it felt like forever – but probably only minutes had passed. He'd seen action movies where the heroes in chains jumped up and twisted to escape their bonds, but the blood made his wrists slippery and he couldn't get the strength.

Another hit, and another, and Felix wasn't letting up. Then he was there using something to cut into Rafe's back.

Rafe's last thought as he fought unconsciousness was about Deacon.

And that he was so damn sorry that Deacon would one day find his body.

CHAPTER 19

Deacon drank his coffee and listened to some guy called Oscar telling him all about what a brilliant teacher Rafe was and how his class of five-year-olds was the most challenging of all.

"Anyway, I don't know how he does it."

Deacon had a reply ready, but was distracted when the main door opened and Mac strode in, followed by a guy in a suit.

"Deacon!" he called, and Deacon made his way over quickly, with sudden fear in his chest. He glanced around for Rafe, but there was no sign of him. He should be back by now.

Mac pulled him aside. "Felix is alive," he said in a low voice.

Deacon reared back, tried to pull away. "I need to find Rafe."

But Mac was shaking him. "It's too late. Felix has Rafe."

Deacon tore himself from Mac's grip. "What? Where?"

"We had Felix in our sights – we didn't know he'd use a baby," Suit said in a whiny, nasal way.

"What?"

Mac moved to stand between Deacon and Suit, holding up a hand. "Feds decided to use Rafe as bait, but they lost Felix."

Deacon acted on pure instinct, bypassing Mac with a smooth move and slamming Suit back against the wall, circling his throat. "What?" he shouted right in the guy's face.

"It was the only way," the man shouted back, and Deacon tightened his grip.

"You knew Felix was here, and you let him get Rafe?"

Mac was at his side. "Let him go, D."

"Fuck that. Where is he?"

"We had the situation u–u–nder control," Suit said, and gurgled and gasped as Deacon decided whether he should just snap the man's neck.

"There's kids here," Mac pointed out, and at that Deacon dropped his hold, Suit falling to the floor.

"I'll have your badge, your life. I'll have you hauled over every single board…" Deacon stopped as he realized he was losing all control and none of this was finding Rafe.

"We had the south exit covered." Suit looked like he was five seconds away from losing his breakfast.

"The tracker – he was wearing Sam's jacket," Deacon snapped. "Let's go."

"The baby is missing," Suit said from the floor, then picked himself up. "As soon as we saw that, we aborted the mission, but it was too late."

"What? Shit, you fuckers."

"We didn't know he was here."

Deacon rounded on the man but said nothing. What was he going to say? What was the point in standing there talking and accusing when Rafe was out there with a fucking psychopath?

"Get in the car, D," Mac insisted. "We have his tracker live and moving."

Deacon's relief was so strong he nearly keeled over with the power of it. He'd never thought they'd be relying on the tracker, because he'd promised he'd keep Rafe safe.

Mac drove at speed as soon as he was out of the town, tailed by a cop car and Evie close behind.

"Ops say the tracker is stationary," Mac said, worry in his tone.

Please don't tell me that. Please don't tell me that Rafe is dead.

In ten minutes flat, they were at the site of the tracker. But there was no Rafe.

Just his jacket, with the tracker in the pocket. Along with a woman and her baby. Anna and Chloe. The baby was wrapped tightly in Rafe's coat, and the woman was covered in blood but alive. For a few seconds, Deacon stared at them, listening to Suit call in paramedics, watching Mac help them up and into Suit's car, and then he realized that what he was looking for wasn't there. Rafe.

"I'll backstop you here," Evie said. "Stay in this area, with the woman and baby."

Deacon nodded mutely. "Tell me there was some other tracker on Rafe. Please."

Mac backed away from him, talking into his earpiece, and Deacon followed, catching some of the words. "...anything... silver Mazda... find it."

"Talk to me," Deacon said, and grabbed at Mac's jacket.

"Tracker has been at this point thirteen minutes. They'll find him," Mac reassured him, and got back in his car, Deacon following. "You armed?"

"Of course I'm not."

Mac reached over and unlocked the gun safe with his thumbprint. "There," he said without added explanation.

Deacon took out the Sig and checked the chamber, then sat back and tried to center himself. "Where are we heading?"

Mac cursed. "Fuck knows."

"What were you even doing in town?"

"Gut instinct," was all Mac said as they peeled away from the spot where Anna and her baby had been left to die. Somehow Mac knew his way, being guided by whoever was talking to him. This nebulous Sanctuary that he worked for. "Then forensics came back. Inconclusive, and camera footage showed a man heading away from the car as it exploded. He was caught in the blast but vanished in the chaos."

"Why didn't you call and tell me?"

Mac shot him a sideways glance. "I was already here. I didn't like this whole situation and I wanted to be here. The news only came in an hour ago."

Deacon shook his head to clear the panic, and instead drew on all his reserves so that he wasn't acting on blind panic but icy resolve.

"Ops lost him here," Mac said, and pulled over to the side of the road. "No satellite coverage cams, nothing, but he's not gone out the other side of the mountain on this road. He's in there somewhere."

Deacon looked up at the peaks, imagined the hundreds of places that Rafe could be with Felix. If he was still alive. Pain knifed through him at the thought. They'd taken years to finally get together, and he wasn't ready to lose Rafe now.

"Okay," Mac said, tapping his ear. "Yeah, I see it. Deacon, get back in the car."

"What do you have?"

"Nothing, maybe, or something."

Deacon subsided and let Mac drive, off the main road and up into the mountains. The directions made little sense, but somehow Mac knew. Deacon didn't ask questions; he just let Mac drive.

"Ops say there is something up here, one of two places. We could be lucky."

Or Rafe could be dead already. He didn't want to think that, but…

"What the hell were the Feds thinking?"

"Felix is a serial killer," Mac said quietly as they followed a straight road at a steep incline. Had Rafe come this way? "You know they'll do anything to get him out of circulation."

"Even putting a civilian's life in danger? If they've got Rafe killed…"

"It's up here," Mac said after more silence. "Ditching the car."

Deacon followed Mac out of the car, and together they sprinted up the remainder of the hill and ducked into the trees. All Deacon could see was a shack, a broken-down building with nothing to show anyone was inside, and then he saw it – the glint of silver. Cautiously but with speed, they made their way to a car. Mac nodded, and Deacon knew it was the right car. Gun high, he indicated he would go around the back of the shack, Mac to the front. Jumping fallen branches and trying to get there as fast as he could, he thought he heard someone scream, and his steps became faster. He skidded to a halt at the back of the shack, the entire wall missing, and for a second he knew he'd fucked up. There was no cover here – nothing except him, trees, and Rafe's broken body held up with chains.

And there, laughing hysterically, with a gun to Rafe's head, was Felix.

"This gets better and better," he said, and grinned. Deacon didn't even think about what he was doing, but he wasn't listening to a fucking monologue or Felix spouting some shit. He shot him. A bullet right in the center of Felix's brain, and he was dead before he hit the floor.

He didn't care about Felix, it was Rafe he was transfixed by, limp and bloody, and Mac helped with the chains until they had Rafe down on the ground.

"Help's on its way," a voice said from the door. Suit, looking at the blood and the chains in shock. "We need to… Jesus… We need help, there's bodies out there."

All Deacon could do was cradle Rafe and try to keep him up off the ground. His breathing was shallow, his back a mess of wounds, his face bloodied, his eyes swollen, and he was unconscious.

"We should take him somewhere."

"EMTs are five out," Mac reassured him.

"We'll want to question him," Suit said. "Is he alive?"

Deacon looked right at Mac. He was going to kill Suit, literally tear him apart with his bare hands. Mac just narrowed his eyes and shook his head subtly.

This isn't the time.

Rafe said nothing. When the paramedic scooped Rafe up and deposited him in the ambulance, he simply climbed in, Mac as well, and then he sat and held Rafe's hand, willing him to wake up.

He didn't know where they were going, where he was being taken. The clinic they arrived at didn't look like a hospital; in fact the paramedic didn't look like any he'd ever seen before, and he finally realized this was the same guy who'd checked Rafe out before. Kieran or something? Some weird name. Kayden, that was it. There was a rough edge to Kayden, but he knew what he was doing. There were no backboards, and if Deacon hadn't known better he would have thought Kayden was carrying out field surgery as he attended to Rafe's wounds.

Mac sat with him, waiting in the hallway outside the closed room, and when Kayden came out he didn't beat around the bush.

"He'll live. Nothing bleeding internally, but you know he'll need watching. Did you get the guy who did this?"

"Yeah," Mac answered for him.

"Good."

"What can I do?" Deacon asked helplessly.

Kayden appeared to consider the question, then with great insight he said, "Understand that he'll have scars."

Mental and physical. And Deacon would be there for him through all of it.

Because all Deacon could think was that scars didn't matter if Rafe was alive.

The first time Rafe opened his eyes, Deacon wasn't there to see it. Kayden found him, told him that Rafe was awake and asking for him.

Deacon was in the room in an instant.

"Anna? The baby?" Rafe's voice was scratchy, and his eyes wouldn't stay open for long. Deacon wanted to go to him, to touch him, reassure himself that Rafe was alive, but he was rooted to the spot.

"Good, all good," he managed. "Anna has a fractured jaw, the baby is completely fine. Anna asked after you. The whole town is asking after you. We kept you out of the papers, but they're reaching for reasons, who you are."

God, stop talking. Why am I still talking? Rafe doesn't need to know all this.

Rafe moved his head and groaned, then muttered something that sounded like Deacon's name.

Deacon moved closer, grasped his hand, held it gently but knowing he didn't ever want to let go. "Do you need something?"

"Say...sorry...need to...for everyone...you."

Deacon's chest tightened. He was trying to apologize to everyone for what? For becoming the target of a man who had killed so many people? There was nothing for Rafe to be sorry about.

"Everything's okay, Rafe."

"It's not," Rafe murmured, and tears slid down his face. He closed his eyes. "It will never be okay."

And all Deacon could do was hold his hand tight until the tears stopped and Rafe was asleep.

CHAPTER 20

Felix Martinez was a serial killer. One of the worst of this century. So far. That was how the news explained the deaths of sixteen people and still rising. *So far* implied that there was worse out there, and Rafe couldn't get his head around that idea. They'd found the three bodies at the shack. Young guys – two were off the streets, the third was just this normal college kid. They'd all been hurt as badly as Rafe and then had their throats cut.

None of that extra bit about how the boys had died was on the bulletins, of course, but he'd pretended to be sleeping so much in the last few days that people had become sloppy around him, and he'd heard more than he should.

As he knew Mac wanted Deacon to work with him for this Sanctuary organization that seemed to help people who were in danger.

As he knew how many men, and women, had died at Felix's hands. He even knew their names from the constantly updated news bulletins.

The connection between him and Felix wasn't made public; he was just an unnamed final victim, and no one knew where he was. It helped that he wasn't in a normal hospital, and to be honest he wasn't entirely sure where he was. The view from the window was of a forest, golden Fall trees, and there wasn't a big changeover in nurses or doctors, so it couldn't be a very big place.

He knew Kayden was there, the same man who had checked him over when Deacon had taken him from the hospital. Kayden knew he was faking sleep, had even called him on it, but he never said anything to Deacon anywhere close enough for Rafe to hear.

And Deacon? He either didn't realize that Rafe was deliberately not opening his eyes, or he was letting Rafe believe he didn't know. Maybe he thought Rafe needed the time to come to terms with everything.

"Hey," a soft voice said to him – a woman's voice. "Are you awake?"

Rafe cracked his eyes a little. Anna was there, and in her arms, Chloe. He opened his eyes the whole way.

"Hey," he said.

Her face was a bruised mess, and he wasn't sure how many days it had been since everything had happened. Five, maybe? He'd lost time in this place; he just knew that the TV stations had moved on from the serial killing to something in politics as the big news item. How long did the murders of so many people deserve to be front-page news? Hell if he knew.

"Thank you," Anna said, and shifted her hold on Chloe.

"I didn't do anything."

She shook her head. "Deacon told me, you left your jacket with that tracker in." She leaned forward. "I won't tell anyone else, I promise. But without that, I'm not sure who would have found us. And my baby…" She trailed away and pressed a kiss to Chloe's head. "Thank you," she said again.

"There's nothing to—"

"Thank you."

Seemed he wasn't going to be allowed to explain that without what he'd done, she and Chloe wouldn't even have been touched. Seemed that no one would let him take any blame. From Kayden, who'd told him to "cut the fucking crap", to Mac, who'd explained that "none of it was your fault; Felix was always a murderer, just like his father before him". Only Deacon let him take the blame, staying deathly quiet when he'd lost control yesterday and told Deacon in no uncertain terms that everything was his fault.

He'd lived, and others had died, and without him poking the hornet's nest, Deacon could have got into the family and taken them down, stopping the killing.

Deacon had shaken his head and left the room, having said nothing at all.

So Rafe knew exactly what Deacon felt. He clearly agreed that this was all on Rafe, and that there was no alternative reasoning.

He talked to Anna for a bit, and tried to hold Chloe, but it was difficult because he couldn't lie back without support for his bandaged back, and his left wrist was broken, yet another limb in plaster. The only bright side was that they'd taken the cast off his leg, and the weirdest thought crossed his mind. If he hadn't had the cast on his leg, would he have been able to kick Felix harder? Would he have gotten away? If he hadn't been so weak, would he have been able to fight back?

The problem was that these thoughts chased into his dreams, and he didn't want them there.

When Anna left, the peace was welcome; at least when the room was empty he didn't have to see pitying looks, or hear reasons why everything was going to be okay.

Sam was one of his regular visitors, armed with grapes and music and a bag of clothes.

"For when you get out," he explained. "We're about the same size, so I grabbed you some of my sweats, and Deacon donated a tee, and the fleece is from Mac, although you realize it will swamp you. Still, it will keep you warm."

That was how Sam's visits went. He talked with great authority on all the news for a good ten minutes, and then he seemed to calm down, and that was the moment when he and Rafe talked the best. Sam was becoming a friend, and they had something in common – they both loved men who couldn't ever sit still.

"So, I was talking to Deacon, and he's worried about you."

"There's no need for him to worry. I'm feeling better every day."

Sue him if he was lying. His back ached, his wrist hurt, his head was filled with scratchy, messy thoughts that he couldn't corral. Sam didn't need to know all that.

"He said he's making things worse, but I managed to calm him down. After he finished punching a wall."

"He punched a wall."

"Went right through the drywall. Fractured a finger, the moron."

"Why would he do that?"

"Why do Deacon or Mac do any of the shit they do." Sam shook his head. "Anyway, I want to tell you about something that… I'm not sure it's the right time…but I have to tell you."

"What? Is Deacon okay?"

"This is nothing to do with Deacon and everything to do with us, because I completely understand survivor's guilt and feeling as if everything that has happened is entirely your fault."

Rafe huffed. "Yeah, right, it just happens that a psycho kidnapped you, tortured you, and killed your parents, not to mention dozens of others as well?" Rafe deadpanned. He was trying for joking, but Sam didn't smile, he shook his head.

"No."

"Then no disrespect, Sam, you're a good guy, but you don't know how I feel."

"When I said no, I meant my story was different. My sister and I were kidnapped when I was a kid, and I was…" He paused, like he was searching for the right word. He even checked behind himself, looking at the shut door. "Tortured, raped, I don't know what you'd call it as a whole."

"Sam. No."

Sam hurried on before Rafe could say anything else. "I don't share the story. It's classified, and there's something about heroes, you know; Mac saved me then, and he kept me alive when we met up again. I had counseling, a lot of it, spent hours in the chair being convinced that I wasn't to blame for what had happened to me. But see… people were telling me it wasn't my fault all that time, and I think if they'd only let me come to that conclusion by myself instead of trying to tell me what to think, then I might have got my head around things a lot quicker."

Sam stopped talking and tilted his head. For a while there was silence, then Rafe felt too uncomfortable with Sam watching him.

"I get that," he said finally, and the admission was one that was easy to make. "Everyone tells me Felix was a killer."

"He was."

"That his dad was as well, my uncle. That it's a family thing."

"You think you're part of it?"

"Why wouldn't I be?"

"Just because your uncle and cousin were… Look, I can't speak for what's in your genetic code or isn't. That's not why I'm here."

"You're here to tell me that I have to come to terms with everything myself. Blah blah."

Sam looked hurt, but then he brightened. "Yeah. That."

"Sorry, I didn't mean to imply—"

"It's cool."

They sat in silence a little longer. Sam was a million miles away, staring out of the window at the trees.

"Deacon left," Rafe said quietly. "I chased him away."

Sam leaned forward, as though he wanted to share a secret. "He's in the hallway. He hasn't moved since you were brought here other than to talk to everyone *about* you. You couldn't chase him away if you were armed with a machine gun and a machete."

Rafe looked past Sam at the closed door. Deacon hadn't given up on him?

"You think you could get him to come in?"

Sam stood up and patted Rafe on the head. "Absolutely."

He left and closed the door behind him, and Rafe realized he should have said something about how sorry he felt for what had happened to Sam; he thought maybe their conversation wasn't entirely done.

But. Deacon.

The man himself was in the room within seconds; he'd clearly been waiting for someone to tell him it was okay for him to go in.

"How are you feeling?" he asked, and hovered by the closed door.

"I'm okay," Rafe lied.

"I know you're lying," Deacon said, and stood behind the chair next to the bed. "May I?" he said, and gestured at the hard plastic seat.

Rafe nodded, but Deacon didn't sit in it in the intended way, he did his usual thing of turning it and straddling it. Rafe couldn't help himself – Deacon doing things like that, sexy things, was enough for him to forget the pain in his wrist.

"What happens now?" Rafe said, vocalizing the mess in his head.

Deacon bit his lip, looking as if he was nervous. "What do you *want* to happen now?"

"Don't do that," Rafe snapped.

"What?"

"The same thing everyone else is doing; tiptoeing around me as if I'm a live grenade and they want to run. I need someone to tell me what the hell happens now."

"You're free to go wherever you want, Rafe. You want to go back to Miami? Because you can. No one is left to hurt you."

"Miami?"

"It's where you lived with your dad. Don't you have a place there?"

"No, we rented. I don't have anywhere."

Except Cambridge Falls and the school. Except anywhere Deacon is.

"Oh, well, I don't know…" He looked fazed, as if he hadn't expected that answer.

Did Deacon *want* him to move away from here, or just away from him, or…hell, where did Deacon even live? Part of him wanted to shut his eyes and lie back on his bed and pretend Deacon wasn't there, but if he did that, then he would never know.

"What would you do if I went to Miami, or stayed in Cambridge Falls, or…I don't know, anywhere?"

"Me?" Deacon looked confused for a second, then the confusion cleared. "That's easy, I'd follow you to wherever you go."

Rafe hadn't been expecting that. "What?"

"I can work from anywhere, really, although there may be times I'm away for stretches, and that would be shit. But that's what a man does. When you love someone, you want them to be where they're happy and you want to be with them."

Okay, so that was intense. Rafe thought about what was in his head that matched his heart right at that moment in time.

"What if I wanted to stay in town, teaching? Do you think they'd have me still?"

"Why wouldn't they? Craig Jenkins has a job for life, I think."

"Yeah, Craig."

"Does it worry you that they won't know you as Rafe? Because you could tell them, everyone."

"Maybe. One day."

"You'll know when it's right."

"And what about you?"

"Me?" Deacon shrugged. "I'd move there with you and buy you your coffee and Danish every morning."

"You make it sound so easy."

"It can be. Not everything is unattainable."

"What will you do?"

"I haven't thought it through. Depends on where I end up, and whether you want me there with you." He stopped and stood, then sat on the side of the bed, perched right on the edge. "Maybe some security work, consulting, possibly even work with Mac. I'll know when it happens. I think I'd like some time just to get my head straight and just be…" he looked out of the window, his expression pensive. "Just be Rafe's partner," he turned back and dimpled a smile. "Or Craig's. I'm easy."

God, yes, he made it sound easy, but Rafe had more obstacles he wanted to put in the way. One of them must trip Deacon up.

"I'd like to stay teaching, as Craig, if they'll have me. I don't want to be connected to what was left of my family; I want time to get my head straight as well."

Deacon held out a hand, which Rafe held tight. "Rafe died," he murmured, then he leaned over and kissed him. "I killed him."

"And Craig?"

"Hell, that's an easy one. I love Craig."

EPILOGUE

Four years later

Chloe decided right at the start of the Halloween party that she was trick-or-treating with Rafe. He and Deacon had become sort of honorary uncles to the little girl, and friends with Anna. Dressed as a cowboy, Deacon was at the back of the small group of kids, all of whom were in Rafe's class this semester. Chloe was dressed as a ballerina, and that was her entire focus since she'd joined the dance school a town over. Rafe took her and Michael, and interestingly enough Billy, who refused to let his family stop him from dancing. Rafe thought Billy was the kind of kid who would live through anything thrown at him and always come out on top. Turned out he'd been right about him and Michael being best friends. Inseparable friends, actually.

He drove them, along with a few other kids from the school. All belted in on the school minibus, which had been a donation from an anonymous benefactor.

Rafe had decided it was Deacon, but his partner, lover and friend had never actually admitted it.

"You don't look much like anything," Chloe informed Rafe when he picked her up.

"I'm a zombie," he said, and threw his hands wide. He hadn't had time to do what he'd really wanted to, because Deacon, the bastard, had been dressed as a cowboy when

Rafe had got home and they'd lost track of time in bed; too late to pick up his outfit.

So Rafe was not Jack Sparrow this year, but, with the addition of quick white face paint, he'd become a zombie teacher. Looked as if it wasn't that convincing, though, because little Chloe just frowned at him.

"Uncle Craig?"

Rafe crouched down to talk to her, his mouth already tilted in a smile. "Wassup, Nina ballerina?"

"I decided I'm gonna marry someone," she said, "like you and Deacon."

Awkward. He and Deacon weren't officially married, although they could be, but they'd never thought much past the whole "my name isn't Craig even though I have all kinds of documentation" thing. They still lived in the apartment over the bakery, had adopted two cats and one three-legged dog. They had Danish for breakfast, so much coffee they kept the shop open single-handed, and loved each other every day. That was enough.

Deacon was happy in his career; he worked freelance with Mac, and was at home more than he was away. The last four years had been a blur, and only when the news had some update on the serial killer case did the memories stir from where Rafe had hidden them away. He still had scars on his back, and his wrist had never quite healed, but he was used to both of those things.

They were nothing compared to being alive.

"That's a really good idea," he said. "Can I come to your wedding?"

"Uh-huh." She leaned in close. "I'm going to marry Billy, or Michael – I haven't decided yet."

Michael must have heard, and from his lofty nearly-ten-year-old height, he looked aghast at the thought. He nudged Billy and whispered something, but Billy didn't look as aghast. He ruffled Chloe's hair, then the two boys ran on to the next house, Chloe flying after them.

The rest of the kids ran to catch up, and Rafe stopped at the beginning of the path to the house, Deacon walking into him, gripping him at the last minute so they didn't both end up on the ground.

"You okay there, hoss?" he asked, drawling the words like some kind of John Wayne; all he was missing was his horse and a six-shooter.

"I love you," Rafe said, clearly but softly.

Deacon's wry smile gave way to a full grin. "I love you too."

"I'd like a Christmas wedding," Rafe murmured, leaning close so this marvelous new plan of his wasn't one he was sharing with the whole town, because what if Deacon stepped back horrified, then maybe laughed at him?

Deacon did neither of those things. He gathered Rafe in and held him close. "A Christmas wedding sounds good."

"Here, in town."

"Yep."

"With Mac and Sam, and everyone here, and the guys you work with at Sanctuary, and the teachers."

"Everyone."

As simply as that, Rafe and Deacon were getting married.

Everyone knew him as Craig in town. No one knew who he really was, only that he was the lucky one who'd escaped a murderer. But that had been a long time ago now.

When the town gathered for the wedding, it was the biggest celebration since last year's Christmas lights switch-on. Sam stood up for Rafe, and Mac was there for Deacon. Chloe got to wear a bridesmaid's dress, and that year's Apple class, along with plenty of other students who had been taught their ABCs by Mr. Jenkins, wore variations on the colors of the rainbow.

The weather was warm, and Rafe was blown away by the love from this town, this place that had been his place to hide out. The wedding was beautiful, the cake delicious, the vows solemn, and the kisses heated.

Rafe knew one thing as Deacon dipped him on the dance floor, laughing like an idiot, with Mac encouraging him from the sidelines.

Craig Jenkins and Deacon Shepherd were going to live happily ever after.

THE END

RJ Scott

RJ's goal is to write stories with a heart of romance, a troubled road to reach happiness, and most importantly, that hint of a happily ever after.

RJ Scott is the bestselling author of over one hundred romance books. She writes emotional stories of complicated characters, cowboys, millionaire, princes, and the men who get mixed up in their lives. RJ is known for writing books that always end with a happy ever after. She lives just outside London and spends every waking minute she isn't with family either reading or writing.

The last time she had a week's break from writing she didn't like it one little bit, and she has yet to meet a bottle of wine she couldn't defeat.

Website: www.rjscott.co.uk
Facebook: https://www.facebook.com/author.rjscott
Twitter: Rjscott_author
Pinterest: pinterest.com/rjscottauthor
Goodreads:
goodreads.com/author/show/3432558.R_J_Scott